Blue Peter

Storytellers

BBC
CHILDREN'S BOOKS

BBC CHILDREN'S BOOKS

Published by the Penguin Group
Penguin Books Ltd, 80 Strand, London, WC2R 0RL, England
Published by BBC Children's Books, 2005

ISBN-13: 978–1–405–90240–3
ISBN-10: 1–405–90240–X

Made and printed in England by Clays Ltd, St Ives plc

Contents

Introduction

Hello there!

Every year, Blue Peter holds big competitions, and every year, it's a tough job to come up with a fresh challenge for our viewers – who always surprise us with their skill and invention.

The idea behind Blue Peter Storytellers was simple enough. Together with our friends at The Arts Council, we invited seven of Britain's top children's authors and illustrators to start a story in words or pictures, which we'd ask our viewers to finish. We're really grateful to our magnificent seven – Malorie Blackman, Raymond Briggs, Lauren Child, Eoin Colfer, Anthony Horowitz, Jacqueline Wilson and David Wood – for agreeing to help inspire our audience.

We launched the competition at the beginning of September. It was the start of a new school term and we knew that homework might have to come first, so we waited for the entries to arrive with bated breath. How many would we get? We needn't have worried. Thousands of emails and sacks of postal entries began to pour into our office. Boxes of them were stacked up everywhere. Everybody on the programme got stuck into reading them – and the standard was so high that we knew that narrowing it down to seven winners and 500 runners-up was going to be an incredibly tough task. Three weeks later, by the closing date of September 30th, we'd read a staggering 33,056 stories. We were all exhausted but it had been such a rewarding task. The stories were sometimes funny, often sad, frequently surprising.

This book is full of the best of them and we'd like to thank our friends at BBC Children's Books for the speed with which they've turned it round. Remember, for every copy we sell, £1 goes to the Blue Peter Treasure Trail Appeal in aid of Childline.

Thank you to everyone who entered and who helped to make this competition such a huge success.

Happy reading!

Richard Marson
Editor, Blue Peter

Konnie, Jacqueline Wilson and Gethin announce the winners live in the Blue Peter studio.

Jacqueline Wilson

Jacqueline Wilson wrote her first 'novel' when she was just nine. Her books include *The Diamond Girls*, *Clean Break* and *Best Friends*, and she has sold over 20 million books in the UK alone! Jacqueline has won many awards, including the Smarties Prize and the Children's Book Award. Her book *The Story of Tracy Beaker* won the 2002 Blue Peter People's Choice Award. Jacqueline is currently the Children's Laureate and the proud owner of a gold Blue Peter badge.

Bradley Escorce-Jones

Bradley is 14 years old and lives in London with his brothers and a cat called Pushkins. His favourite Blue Peter pet is Meg because she's cute. The writers who Bradley admires are Jacqueline Wilson, JK Rowling and Lemony Snicket. He loves cooking, writing, art and drama. Of writing *Golden Feather!* he said, "I enjoyed letting my imagination go wild. It was difficult when I got writer's block and didn't know where to go next."

Golden Feather!

Bradley Escorce-Jones and Jacqueline Wilson

Chapter 1
The Dream

I've never been so frightened in my life! I don't know what to do. I've just got to keep very very still. One wobble and I'm done for. I can't even cling to anything. My fingernails scrabble but there's no groove in the brickwork, no ledge, no creeper. Plain brick wall behind me. Yawning space in front. I mustn't look! Yet my eyes swivel and just for one second I peer down down down. My stomach lurches. I feel as if it's about to spill right out of me. I take a deep breath. I can't be sick now! I've got to think what to do. If only I was a cartoon child I could pedal in the air, my trainers whirring like helicopter propellers. I concentrate on my shoulder blades, willing them to sprout wings. No use. Not so much as a feather. I've got to be brave. But I'm the wuss who can't even watch **Dr Who** *without getting nightmares. Get me out of this nightmare, please!*

I keep having this same vision, over and over again. No one will listen to me, though. If only I could figure out what being stranded on a window sill means, then maybe this would all stop and I could finally get in a decent night's sleep. I've tried and I've tried, but nothing seems to make any sense at all.

It all started a couple of months ago on my thirteenth birthday; I was so excited about becoming a teenager. I went everywhere, to the cinema, water sports and even to one of London's top restaurants. Just before I was about to return home, I stopped off at a Mystic and Magic shop; it looked really cool, so I couldn't help having a look.

At the back of the shop there were a pair of shimmering purple curtains, underneath which a flashing light emerged. Being the nosey person that I am, I couldn't resist having a look. How very stupid I was. As I opened the curtains my body lost all control. I was flung forward and ended up in a pitch-black empty room. Suddenly a light emitted from a crystal ball on a small table. As that was all I could see, I went towards it. The blinding light bemused my eyes. I put my hands on top of the crystal ball to shield my eyes from the beams of light. That was the first time I saw the dream, and in a matter of seconds I was returned to the shop. Nothing else happened that day but every night thereafter it has been repeating through my mind.

Oh, by the way, my name's Michael, Michael Roberts!

Chapter 2
The Chosen One

Get me out of this nightmare, please!

See, I told you: night after night this is what has been happening. The funny thing is that I always wake up at the exact same spot. Over breakfast I thought a bit more about this situation. I reckon I'll go back to the Mystic and Magic shop, I mean, how often can someone be transported into a completely different room by opening a pair of curtains? The best time to go is probably after school, providing I don't get a stupid detention or something.

"Michael, hurry up, or you'll miss the bus!"

That's my mum, Juliana, she's quite bossy but she's doing it for my well-being and that's the main thing.

"Okay Mum, see you tonight."

"Bye. Love you."

"Yeah, yeah."

I hope I can finally figure out what's wrong with me, and I want to do it myself, not end up at a psychiatrist.

There's the bus. I better get on, don't want to be late now do I?

I go to St Michael's School for Boys, funny, isn't it, St *Michael's*? Our head teacher Mr Bromwell is so stupid, I mean he's practically brain-dead, and that's not me just being mean. Look, if we're all playing outside at break, he watches us out of his gigantic window. Even though he can see us clearly, all we can see are a pair of googly eyes and a pointed, crooked nose, not to mention the fact that he has no hair.

He looks like a complete loser. Umm, don't actually tell him I said that, or I'll be in detention for weeks, listening to his awful plans on child safety:

"All pupils need to be equipped with helmets and shin pads when running to prevent damage when stumbling."

Or:

"While swimming lessons are taking place all students must ensure they carry a full oxygen tank to prevent drowning."

My school is so old, the teachers were probably here when they were kids, now that's prehistoric! The brickwork is covered in grime, and all the wooden frames around the windows and doors are rotting away. I'm surprised Mr Bromwell doesn't think they'll fall down. I wish he would close the school, that would be wicked!

"Attention all students."

Oh what a surprise, it's Mr Bromwell with all his Monday morning announcements. Yippee!

"It has come to my attention that the school is now of an age at which it needs refurbishing. Therefore the school will be closed for the rest of the week. Please leave the premises in an orderly fashion from your nearest exit."

Result! A whole week off school, now I've got more time to explore the shop.

Hey, didn't I say that I wanted the school to close, so how – ? No, it was just a coincidence – nothing more.

As I went through the school gates I saw something shocking, so shocking that I almost fainted. There in front of me was the window sill, the same one that I was stranded on in my dream. The tree's there, the roof's the same, it looks, like, like identical.

No, it can't be, not here, it's just my mind playing tricks on me. I turned on my heels and sprinted home, I didn't look behind me just focussed straight ahead. I had to get back to that shop; things were getting weirder by the second.

"Hi Mum, guess what?"

"Aren't you a bit early?"

"Yeah, school's off for a week!"

"Why's that then?"

"'Cause it's getting refurbished."

"Okay, make sure you do your homework."

"Yeah, yeah. By the way, I'm going out to the shops."

"Are you asking me, or telling me?"

"Sorry, can I go to the shops?"

"If you hurry. Aunt Katrina's coming in a hour."

"Okay, I'll try not to get lost and not come back."

"Michael!"

"Sorry. Bye."

I arrived at the shop about 15 minutes later, panting and out of breath. I walked up to the door, a sign hung in the window. As I looked at it I read, 'Closed for refurbishment'. Closed for refurbishment, first school, now this. What's going on?

Just as I turned around to head home, I saw something glisten from under a plant pot. I'd seen this in movies, you know, people leaving spare keys under plant pots. My instincts told me to go after it, maybe I was meant to see it and go in. I picked it up and bent over the lock. As I inserted it into the keyhole a small tingling sensation grew right through me.

No use, it wouldn't budge.

Oh, I wish it would open!

A clunking sound emerged from the lock as the door swung open. But how–? It must have been a delay. But that's the second time today. No, no, just coincidence. I strolled in casually so nobody outside would get suspicious. The lights weren't on so I couldn't see, but as I rotated, to no surprise of mine, a flashing light appeared from behind a pair of illuminated curtains. I went forward to touch the curtains but nothing happened, nothing at all.

What a waste of a day. I was turning to leave, when suddenly I realized the shop had gone. Two empty chairs replaced it. Even though nobody was there I sat down, got comfortable and waited for something to happen.

BANG!

I jumped and screamed as suddenly an old woman appeared in the other chair.

"Silence, child, it is only me, Madame Lou Lou."

"Madame Who Who?"

"Don't be foolish, child. You heard me."

"Who are you?"

"I just said!"

"No, who exactly are you?"

"Michael, my dear child, I am your Guardian, your Conscience, your other Soul."

I froze.

"How do you know my name?"

"Everyone knows your name – Chosen One."

"Chosen One? Is that code for lunatic?"

"No, you have been chosen by the gods to rid the ParraWorld of evil."

"Yeah, of course, and I'm a dragon coming to eat you, HA HA!"

"Gods are serious matters. DO NOT treat them with sarcasm."

"Right, because I really believe you, your so-called gods are probably some other insane people, like you, in costumes."

"HOW DARE YOU? Never insult the gods. Never, do you hear me? NEVER!"

A ring of fire ignited around my chair and Madame Lou Lou disappeared. A winged beast emerged from the flames.

I was trapped, and doomed.

"Help, please! Help!"

All went dark again and Madame Lou Lou returned in a bad temper.

"Hasn't anything weird happened lately?" she said.

"Well yeah, but it was just coincidence."

"No, no, no, Chosen One, not at all, it is true, you are enriched with power."

"Okay, you say what you like, but just let me go home."

"Once you have listened, of course I will let you go. You have been chosen to accept The Quest, a quest that will change the worlds."

"I'm not accepting any stupid quest, no matter what."

"You have no choice. It's your destiny. You will accept."

"Okay, Okay, OKAY, I've had enough. LET ME GO!"

"As you wish, Chosen One! BEGONE!"

Chapter 3
An Early Wake-up Call

I was transported back to my room. It had to have been a dream. I couldn't be the Chosen One, could I? So many thoughts were racing through my head. I don't know what to believe anymore. I wish I'd never gone back to the shop. Why am I so curious? No wonder Aunt Katrina always says, "Curiosity killed the cat." Now I understand what she means.

I told my best friend Matthew about the shop, well I tried. Halfway through he burst out laughing and ran off to tell everyone. Now they all think I'm a nutter.

School's arranged an Outdoor Education Trip to make up for the time that we can't go into class. Even though we will probably end up in a skanky pit with spiders and woodlice, it should still be fun.

"Michael, am I taking you, or are you going with Matthew?"

Why would I want to go with that bin bag?

"Can you take me Mum? Matthew's car broke down and he's taking a train."

"Okay. Be ready in five. I'll wait in the car for you."

Yes! She fell for it, no more Matthew McDouglas. Well, at least until we get there.

Hey, if I'm the Chosen One what happens if I wish he was injured? No, that's too unfair. But I could – no, not that either.

I arrived at the Royal London Camping Academy at about five to six. The rest of the class were all bunched together in a circle. As I walked round to join them, I heard a couple of sniggers and bits of mumbling. No points for guessing who they're aimed at.

"Great, now that we're all here we can get on with tent and room allocations. Here's how it'll work. We have two buckets, names of boys in one and 'R' for rooms or 'T' for tents in the other. So three names will be picked out of one bucket, then they will pick for a room or a tent."

That's Miss Smith, she's basically Mr Bromwell's clone. Wait, nobody can get that dumb.

Maybe I shouldn't be so mean. Anyway, look on the bright side, there's a nine in ten chance that I won't be with Matthew.

"So boys... Uh-hum, William, you'll be sharing with... Matthew and... Michael."

What? Nine in ten, nine in ten, how on earth did that happen? Nine in ten. Probability is worthless.

"Oh great, we're stuck with Psycho Kid!"

"Shut it William."

"Now, now, boys, NO arguments."

"Yes, Miss Smith."

We were sent off to our sorry excuse for a room. Royal London, how can this be classed as Royal? The lights are blown, the mirror's cracked, the door's hanging off one hinge and the bed springs are completely out of place. I couldn't be bothered to have any sort of conversation with the two traitors that I once called friends, so I jumped into my pyjamas and settled down to sleep.

******

Get me out of this nightmare, please!

An eerie sound brought me upright in my bed. It began to grow louder and louder, closer and closer. I called for Matthew and William. No answer. I shouted, still no answer. The sound broke out into a shivering wail; I couldn't take any more. I couldn't see and I was experiencing a deafening sound. I screamed. An echoing laugh silenced me; there at the side of my bed were Matthew and William, both in hysterics.

"Ha, ha, Psycho's gone mad again, seeing ghosts again are we? Ooooooooooooooo, look I'm a ghost, ooooooooooooooo."

"Right, I've had enough of your games, Matthew."

If I am the Chosen One then he's really in for it now. I focussed my eyes on Matthew. In a split second the broken light reignited and sparks began to fly everywhere. Suddenly the framing broke away and knocked Matthew straight in the face and sent him flying to the floor.

Blood began to pour everywhere. I'm the one who's in for it now.

Chapter 4
Another Encounter

Wow! I never thought I had those kind of powers; maybe I am some sort of Chosen One.

But what about that quest?

I was removed from the camp earlier, due to unacceptable behaviour. At least it wiped the smile off Matthew's face.

I'm supposed to be grounded for a month but it's my aunt's birthday and we're going out for dinner.

"Michael, hurry up, we're going to be late!"

"Okay, Mum, I'm just trying to find my shoes."

"I want to see you in the car in five minutes, do you hear me?"

"Yes, Mum."

She's become really strict lately just because of the incident.

We arrived at the Restaurante Delicio on time that evening, which is quite good seeing as we're always late. Aunt Michelle was waiting at our reserved table as we entered. After about 15 minutes of meaningless conversation, a disturbing cough came from behind.

"Uh-hum. Please may I have your order?"

"Yes, I'll have…"

"No, no, you must order from our children's menu, there is a special competition you should enter."

I turned round to accept the children's menu.

"Hey! Aren't you that Madame person from the Mystic and Magic shop?"

"No, I'm just a waitress at the Restaurante Delicio,

here to take your order. You should enter the competition you know, it will do you the world of good."

"I'll think about it, but are you sure that you're not…"

"As sure as I'll ever be, now can I take your order?"

I ordered my usual Pizza Margherita; it was good, even though I finished it in a matter of minutes.

"Michael, my dear, aren't you going to enter that competition? That lady was so eager for you to try it."

"Okay!"

It was a bit easy. All I had to do was pick three numbers that added up to 13, and sort out a puzzle. I walked up to the reception desk and rang the bell to get someone's attention. No response. I rang again. An old woman came up from behind the desk.

"Hi, Madame Lou Lou!"

"Sorry, I know not of a Madame Lou Lou, how may I help?"

"Yeah, here's the competition entry you asked me to do."

"I never asked for an entry but thank you."

She strolled over to a computer and entered in my details.

"Congratulations, you are a winner. Here is your prize, use it well and let your imagination take control."

POOF!

She disappeared in a flash and all that was left was a small golden box addressed to 'The Chosen One'. I turned around to see if anyone was looking, but everyone else was too involved with his or her food to take any notice of what I was doing.

I opened the box and inside laid a golden feather on a golden chain, with a piece of old parchment containing a map by its side. I placed the chain around my neck and stuffed the paper into my pocket. As I returned to the table Mum was already getting ready to go, so we said our goodbyes and headed off home.

Chapter 5
An Imaginative Guide

The second of our outside school trips is taking place today. We're going to the Science Museum, and funnily enough science is my worst subject. Mum had practically to beg the school to let me go, but I'm not surprised that they didn't want a violent pupil to come along.

After a long discussion they finally allowed me onto the bus, and we set off for the Science Museum. Outside it looked like a thousand-year-old castle, but inside it was so modern that we felt we'd travelled into the future. We were told to pair up so that nobody would get lost, they called it 'The Buddy System'!

Surprise, surprise, I was on my own, so the school decided to put me with a guide. I wandered over to the guide collection area with my ticket. A bald-headed man rather like Mr Bromwell took my ticket.

"Number 13, guide number 13."

From behind the desk came another Madame Lou Lou lookalike. Even though she would never admit it, I still believed it was her and that she was stalking me.

"Hi, my name is Professor Parkinson, may I ask yours?"

"Hi, I'm the Chosen One, but you should know that shouldn't you, Madame Lou Lou?"

"Who is Madame Lou Lou? I am Professor Parkinson, and what's your real name?"

"Michael."

We wandered around for about two hours looking at

exhibits, from the solar system to the invention of the steam train. I enjoyed the space simulation most; it really felt like you were in a spacecraft flying up, down and all around. I quite enjoyed the 'GROSS' section as well; there were bogey and earwax machines, even slime that fell from the ceiling.

We stopped off for lunch just before we were meant to meet up with the others. I enjoyed a beefburger with fries accompanied by a strawberry milkshake. As I went across to the toilets, Professor Lou Lou whispered into my ear, "Let your imagination take control." Before I could reply she had pushed me into the toilets and bolted the door behind me.

What did she do that for? After I had finished with the toilet, I went to wash my hands but then I found there were no towels to dry my hands with. I reached into my pockets in search of a tissue. The map of the museum fell from my pocket and managed to glide to the other side of the room. From a distance it showed a pattern that looked rather familiar. It looked like the map from the restaurant!

I was meant to be here, I just knew it. I pulled the other map out from my pocket and had a closer look. So, if the centre of the museum is the elevator to the space rocket simulator, then that is my best ticket to the ParraWorld.

I ran to the door and attempted to open it. It was sealed shut, no use.

I had worked out too much to waste it all now. I concentrated hard on the door; an electrical energy surged through me. Suddenly my golden feather began to glow. A loud clicking sound was emitted from the door as it flew straight off its hinges. Before anyone could see me I sprinted off towards the space simulation. I was the only one in the area so I got in almost immediately.

Problem. How do I use it? There were 12 floors, well 13, but it looked like you needed a key to get to the top floor. That's it, a key. I pulled out my feather and slotted it into the keyhole. One 90° turn and then the elevator started to shake. After about 30 seconds it stopped dead. The door squeaked open and a blinding light filled the lift.

I was weightless, flying through thin air.

Chapter 6
The Never-ending Tunnel

I felt like being sick. I couldn't take it any more. Luckily I finally landed in a red and golden throne encrusted with carvings of the golden feather. Scurrying feet came from the nearby corridor. I heard a few cries of, "He's here!", "Finally our saviour!" and, "Hurray! We're saved!"

"Presenting King Parrathon The Eighth of ParraWorld."

"Greetings, Chosen One, glad you found your way."

"So, can you fill me in on this quest?"

"Of course. You have been chosen by the gods to defeat the evil Lord Zarron, and save the rest of the ParraWorld."

"So how do I find and destroy him?"

"Well that is why you are Chosen, it is written that you and only you can do just that."

"So I have no guidance from you whatsoever?"

"Well, all I can say is, 'Let your imagination take control'."

"I guess I better be off then. Goodbye."

"Farewell, dear child. Farewell."

******

I searched for hours, but there was no sign of an entrance to an evil lair. Nothing seemed to give the slightest clue either.

I couldn't carry on with this without a rest, so I sat

down on a nearby rock and relaxed for a while. I looked out to the horizon. The sun was just starting to set, so it made quite an inspirational view. I looked up at the sky; a row of identical clouds all circulated around my head, nothing special though, just blobs here and blobs there.

"Let your imagination take control."

Wait a second! They're not blobs, they're arrows pointing behind me! I turned around, and there in front of me was a blocked archway made out of fish fossils. My feather began to glow again; I focussed on the archway and walked straight ahead.

This was either going to work, or hurt very much. I carried on and didn't even feel a thing; it was an illusion and nothing more. I found myself in a dark, twisted cave with jagged rocks hung from the ceiling. There was no way I was standing in the same place for more than a minute while an evil lord was around, so I began to make a move.

The tunnel twisted and turned, went uphill and downhill but carried on no matter what. I began to think I was going around in circles, my surroundings were so similar. I reached into my pocket and pulled out my map. It had worked in the museum, maybe it would work here. There was nothing significant about the tunnel apart from the rocks, so I had a closer look at them.

Hang on a second, these weren't ordinary rocks: they were all identical, too identical if you ask me. I touched the nearest one. It began to shiver and eventually broke off. Suddenly it turned into a stone gargoyle: a winged creature made entirely of rock. It began to approach me; carelessly, it began to fire crystal blue energy balls from its mouth in every direction.

I had an idea, if I made more of these gargoyles appear then maybe they would destroy each other.

I concentrated on the space around me. The tunnel started to shake; one by one the jagged rocks fell and more gargoyles appeared. In the confusion they all began to fire at each other. Energy balls flew everywhere, wings flapped wildly, and dust rose from every nook and cranny. Shattering sounds were all that could be heard. It was working.

As all the dust settled, what looked like a demolition site began to be revealed. Suddenly the tunnel walls began to break away, and were replaced by brick walls just like any house. I followed the corridor right to the end. There was a large oak wooden door with lion-shaped knockers.

The doors opened, but nothing could prepare me for what I was about to encounter.

Chapter 7
The Day of Reckoning

The doors swung open revealing a stone path with lava flowing on either side. At the end of the path sat a fireplace, or rather a 'lavaplace', because this was the mouth of the stream. It pumped out vigorous amounts of this molten liquid, causing flames to erupt around it.

I was walking closer to examine the fireplace when suddenly the door slammed shut. There in front of it stood a hideous hooded figure. Glowing red eyes were all that could be seen under its hood.

"So, Chosen One, we finally meet. I am Lord Zarron."

"We finally do, and I'm here to stop you from causing any more pain and suffering to the people of the ParraWorld."

"Please don't make me laugh. You will fall, like every other child that has ever faced me."

"You won't defeat this Chosen One."

He began to laugh louder than ever as he fell to the floor. He started to glow. What was going on? He had transformed. His figure changed completely. All that was in front of me was the thing I feared most.

An anaconda began to slither towards me. I stepped back.

"You ssssee, the only way to overcome a fear is to facccce it. That proves you're as weak as the rest."

He transformed back.

"Don't you wonder why someone as powerful as me

would have lava in their palace? It's because I'm a fighter: someone who overcomes things."

"No. Because you're a creep."

"Hand me your golden feather, and let me absorb your energy."

"I will never give in to you."

"Then you shall DIE!"

What should I do? I don't know how to fight against an evil lord. He raised his arm and took hold of an invisible tube. That tube happened to be my throat. I couldn't breathe; he was much stronger than I, with no effort at all. I needed a plan. I needed to fight back. I conjured two rocks out of the lava and fired them at Zarron.

He let go, but I wasn't safe yet.

"So, you can use your powers. But let's see how well. TAKE THAT!"

I was thrown backwards by an invisible force. The force of impact caused me to become paralyzed.

ZAP, ZAP, ZAP!

I was hit with an energy ball; it seemed to be all over, so soon. He walked straight over me and turned back to look down upon me.

"So weak, so worthless, so pathetic."

"But I'm too young to die."

Why did that come out? I didn't know what to say, but anything was better than that.

"Michael Roberts – you're never too young to die."

I was in for it now. What could I possibly do? I needed a plan and it had to come quick.

Didn't he say that he feared lava and fire, could that be his weakness?

I had no other options, it was now or never. I concentrated hard on the stream, suddenly the lava began to bubble, bubble so high that it created a wave. The wave flew over the path knocking Zarron clean off his feet and into the other side of the stream. I had done it; I had defeated Zarron. I WAS THE CHOSEN ONE!

Something flew out of the stream, landing straight onto the path. A robotic structure of a human was blocking my way.

"Lord Zarron will not be defeated that easily."

The machine stayed alight as it moved closer, it started as a walk, then a jog and finally progressed into a run. I was only human and it would send me flying. Unless…

I looked up and saw a couple of sprinklers placed along the ceiling; under one of them stood a pillar. I focussed on the top of the pillar and felt myself being lifted towards it. One cool thing that I did see in the Science Museum was what happened when super-hot metal is cooled down quickly.

How could I set the sprinkler off though? I removed my feather.

"Hey Zarron, if you want it come and get it."

He rose from the ground and landed directly in front of me.

"Zarron, here's a science lesson for you: what happens when heated metal is cooled at a rapid rate?"

The heat was so intense that it set off the sprinklers. BLEEP, BLEEP, BLEEP, BLEEP, BLEEP, BLEEP, BLEEP, BLEEP, BLEEP, BLEEP!

Water rained down upon him.

"NOOOOOOOOOO, you didn't, you couldn't have, NOOOOOOOOOO!"

"Greed doesn't get you anywhere, bye bye now."

I pushed him over the side of the pillar; he shattered into millions of pieces as he hit the floor. It was all over; what seemed like forever was finally over. I had done what was needed for the good of mankind.

The day of reckoning was finally upon us.

Chapter 8
A Safe Journey Home

An eerie spirit rose from Zarron's remains. As his soul floated up to me, I froze. My feather began to glow again, but this time it started to hurt me.

Zarron began to spin around; a tornado was what replaced him. The tip of the tornado floated around me and into my feather. Suddenly my feather became a vortex-like portal sucking up the rest of Zarron.

I was left alone. How was I going to get out? Could I teleport? Did I have that sort of power?

I felt weightlessness again, and eventually I found myself back at King Parrathon's palace.

I never teleported, so who did?

"Congratulations, dear child, you have restored peace to the ParraWorld and have rid it of the greatest of evil."

"Thanks, but can you tell me something? What did having the dream mean?"

"Well, dreams are the only way in which the ParraWorld can contact your world, we sent it to you as a message that something was wrong."

"And when I defeated Zarron, a tornado-like object went into my feather, what was that?"

"Simply Zarron's powers being transported to you. You see, when a significant person is defeated then the victor will always receive their powers."

"So I guess I'll head home now. Oh no, I've been gone for hours, school will realize that I'm missing."

"No, do not fret dear child, Madame Lou Lou has

30

made sure your disappearance has gone unnoticed."

"Okay, thanks for everything."

"No, Michael. Thank *you*."

"Uh, how do I get back?"

"Let your imagination take control!"

I was lifted to my room, where I lay and thought about the day's events. At first I had thought that I was going crazy, but then I had faced Lord Zarron and proved to myself that I truly was the Chosen One.

It had been quite a hectic day, what with me running about and everything. I lay there for a couple of minutes, then finally sent myself to sleep reminiscing about the day.

******

Hey! I'm cured, no dreams, no visions, I'm FREE!

Chapter 9
Another Call

After a few weeks things started to get back to normal. Even though I had to lie to everyone, telling them that I was just having a laugh about my powers, it was worth it. It took most people about two to three days to believe me, but Matthew and William took a lot longer. Who could blame 'em! After being trapped in a room with a super-powered kid who hated you at that particular moment, wouldn't you be a bit scared?

Things at home started to liven up too. Mum met a new bloke at one of her bingo nights, and now they're going to salsa classes regularly. I was a bit uncomfortable with it at first, but after he bought me the latest games console and a whole selection of games I soon got used to him. Hey! Who said bribery doesn't work?

It's a bit of a shame that my adventure is all over, even though it was tough. But guess what? I still have all my powers. I should be a superhero ridding London of all EVIL!

I'll have a superhero name too... what about... Super Kid? Nah, that's a bit babyish, umm... I know! Golden Feather. Yeah, that's right. I'm Golden Feather, here to fight crime and save the world! The only problem is that all superheroes need to have disguises – and Halloween's months away.

But I know Madame Lou Lou should be able to conjure up something special for me.

I spent all night working on my suit; I went through hundreds of designs, but only one felt right. I teleported to Madame Lou Lou and gave her my ideas. She made it almost instantly. It's like it jumped out of the paper and onto my body.

"Just use your powers to change back into your normal clothes."

"Thanks, see you around."

I span round and changed back into my everyday clothes. It was wicked. It was a dream come true. I fell asleep almost instantly that night, no worries at all. Life was great.

******

Get me out of this nightmare, please!

Oh no, not again. Wait a second! That means they're in trouble.

Looks like the real adventure is just beginning.

"Don't worry ParraWorld, Golden Feather's here to save the day!"

The End... or is it?

Eoin Colfer

Photograph © Susan Greenhill

A former primary school teacher, Eoin Colfer is the award-winning author of 12 books. In 2000 he cast a spell on the publishing and film industries with his fantastically original novel *Artemis Fowl*, and hasn't looked back since. The fourth book in the hi-tech, hi-spec Artemis Fowl adventures was published in May 2005.

Beth Wright

Beth is 14 and lives in Wiltshire with her younger brother and two cats, called Felix and Simba, a couple of gerbils and lots of fish. She enjoys reading Chris D'Lacey, Eoin Colfer and Michael Morpurgo. Beth loves chocolate and spending time with her family, friends and pets. Of writing *The Blue Army*, she said, "I most enjoyed making up the setting – the Freeland and Borderland – because I could let my imagination run wild."

The Blue Army

Beth Wright and Eoin Colfer

KC still remembered how blue the sky had been on that day. At that precise moment. It's funny what the brain decides to remember in greatest detail. You would think, perhaps, that KC's brain would have taken a mental snapshot of the million metallic shards flying all around in a deadly hail. Or maybe the mysterious army in the glowing blue armour that had appeared from nowhere, destroying everything in range of their combat rifles. That would have been worth remembering, surely. But no. KC was surprised to find that those images had faded somehow. What remained was the blueness of the sky. Perhaps KC's subconscious had realized that a war was coming, and the sky would not be quite so blue for a long time.

There were three things that KC remembered about his life before the war. One was his name: Keitaro Michelangelo Claudius Brown. But no one called him Keitaro. No one dared call him Michelangelo. No one called him Claudius. And if anyone called him Keitaro Michelangelo Claudius, then they were either very brave, or very foolish. More commonly the latter.

KC had never forgiven his mother for that. That little joke that she thought would be funny, when he was born, 14 years previously, had turned very bitter, very quickly. As soon as he was old enough to realize the burden that his name caused, he had dropped the M completely and took his other initials to form his preferred title – KC.

The second thing that he remembered was his mother, Karin Brown. He remembered the tone of her sweet singing, that echoed inside the giant glassy Domes of their home in the heart of the Freeland Plains. He could recall the joyous notes that she would sing to herself when she was happy and, when KC himself was upset or down, the long, melancholy notes that she'd sing to him. The songs weren't here now. And neither was she. No Freelanders at all. There was no one now. There was no one to sing beautiful songs to him when he woke up in the night, crying out for comfort – which happened often. His mother had been just one of the many Freelander innocents who had fallen to the rifles of the Blue Army. His mother was gone for good, and he didn't remember his father at all.

The last scrap of information that KC remembered was not so much from before the war, as from the beginning of the war itself. It was this sliver of information that was most prominent of all. It was foremost in his mind in his waking hours, and the subject of his dreams during those hours that he spent sleeping. The blue of the sky. That was what he remembered. The bright blue of the sky that he could see inside and outside the Freeland Domes, beneath which he had lived his whole life. His whole life before the war.

KC couldn't see the blue now. He could see white. The white of the bedsheets, the white of the spotless walls, and the white of the scrubbed floors. Even the ceiling was white steel. The ceiling. It was closing in on him – or at least he felt as if it was. In the Freeland Domes, the ceilings had been high, high up, and made of a shimmering transparent metal, so above the blue sky was visible. Now, KC felt swamped in white, claustrophobic. It was all so new to him. There'd been no white in Freeland. Freeland had been colourful, Freeland had been happy, Freeland had been – there was no other way to describe it – free. The refugee centre wasn't free. It was a prison. No one was allowed out into the big city unaccompanied, and no one was allowed in apart from on pre-arranged visits. And no one came to see KC. So he was left alone, drowning in the whiteness of the ward.

He instinctively closed his deep emerald eyes so as not to see the white. The darkness took him immediately and he felt his consciousness begin to slip away. He was off into dreamland.

******

The day dawned fine. The sun rose slowly in the east, the huge Freeland Domes casting long shadows over the Freeland Plains. KC was up early that day. He was up early every day. He liked to watch the sunrise in the early morning. If he screwed up his eyes really tight, he could see a tiny sliver of blue that was the sea in the distance. Slowly, ever so slowly, the sun would rise over that thin sliver, lighting first the distant sea, making it glitter and sparkle, then the nearer Borderland state and eventually Freeland itself. It took about an hour in total. And after that hour, KC usually felt ready to begin the day.

It was the sky that attracted KC's attention that day. Its blue was quite overpowering. There were no clouds. Not even the tiny wispy clouds that played across the sky, casting shadows on the heat-baked soil of Freeland and Borderland far below. KC lay flat on his back, outside his Dome, watching the sky.

He wasn't just out here to watch. It was also to get away from the whispers. The gossip. The words that were passing from Freelander to Freelander about the coming invasion. There would be an invasion – of that everyone was sure – but why, no one could say. It was KC's job to patrol the Border. It had been since news of the invasion had spread to the Freeland Domes, two weeks before. Since then, every day from half past five in the morning until four in the afternoon, it was KC's responsibility to keep a look out for the invaders from across Borderland. He was glad that he'd been given the morning shift. He hadn't fancied patrolling the freezing wastes of the Border in the dead of night – that was the time when the hyenas and the jackals came out to play.

KC looked at his watch. It was 5:28am. Regretfully he picked himself up and grabbed his shoulder bag that contained his lunch. He swung it over his head and set off for the border. It was about 15 minutes' walk from the Domes to the Border so he'd be late, but KC didn't hurry. He knew that his predecessor,

Jacob Stepping, would stay on until he arrived. Jacob was like that.

After about two minutes, KC looked behind him. He could see the three Freeland Domes towering above him – the only landmark for miles and miles around. He could see the tiny figure of a tall lady with long blonde hair flowing down her back standing inside the Secondary Dome, by the wall, waving to him. KC smiled. It was his mother. He waved back and turned around to begin walking again. Karin was always there when he left in the mornings, waving him off. She was always there in the afternoon when he returned, welcoming him back with a steaming stew or soup for his tea.

This thought carried him to the Border. The Border. It wasn't much. Just a small ditch in the earth with a thin wire fence surrounding it. No barbed wire, no alarms, no searchlights. But to Borderlanders and Freelanders alike it meant so much. Barbed wire, alarms and searchlights simply weren't needed. It was a divide between states; between whole ways of life.

Jacob was a small figure in the distance. KC tried to shout, but Jacob couldn't hear. Sighing, he threw his lunch down at the side of the ditch and ran after him. When he was 20 feet away, Jacob must have heard his footfalls, for he turned around and beamed when he saw KC.

"KC! I thought you'd never turn up! It's gone twenty to six," he said, smiling at his friend.

"Yeah, sorry, Jacob. I lost track of time… I'll make it up to you tomorrow, honest. So, how was your shift?"

"Boring. Nothing more than one lonely hyena."

KC made a face and Jacob laughed. "I don't know why you're scared of them, KC Brown. They don't do anything but laugh manically."

"I'm not scared of them!" KC bristled.

Jacob threw a playful punch at him. "Yeah?"

"'Course."

Jacob shrugged. "Well, whatever," he replied. "I'm starving. See you later, KC."

Jacob turned backwards and picked up his empty lunch bag and heavy night overcoat from the ditch. He donned his bag and tied his coat around his waist – it was far too hot, even in the early morning, to wear such a garment with the sun up. He waved at KC and jogged away back to the Domes where his breakfast was awaiting him.

KC watched his friend out of sight, then turned back to the east, in the direction of Borderland. He could see the sea in the distance but other than that, nothing but the sun-drenched Borderland scrub. There were no Domes on the Borderland Wastes. No one knew where the Borderlanders lived. It was a running joke among Freelanders that Borderlanders were primitive enough to live in tunnels and caves underground, like rabbits or badgers. But often, KC wondered whether that really was where Borderlanders lived. After all, there was no evidence of civilization anywhere else in Borderland, and it was a well-known fact that the whole of Borderland could be seen from the Border. It was one of the many things that Freelanders boasted about among themselves.

KC settled down to watch. Strictly speaking, he should begin to pace the border. Up and down. Up and down. And for the first few days on patrol, KC had. Back then, he'd taken his duties very seriously. He'd never had a job before and he was honoured that so much trust had been put in him. But soon, as each day crept by without sign of the imminent invasion, KC's vigilance had slipped somewhat. So now, a fortnight after he had first been given the post, KC spent most of his shift just sitting and admiring the view. Perhaps it was laziness, he never saw Jacob sitting down on the job – but all that walking wasn't really necessary, was it?

An hour slipped by. And another. The sun climbed higher in the sky, and it became steadily hotter. Occasionally KC would stand up, move about a bit, perhaps walk 500 metres further down the border and then sit back down again.

It was almost half past ten before anything unusual happened. At first KC was sure that his eyes were playing tricks on him. Or that it was one of those famous mirages that he'd heard so much about from the Hunters when they came back from a trip onto the Freeland Plains on a particularly hot day. But no matter how much KC rubbed his eyes, or moved up and down the Border, looking at the mirage from different directions, it stayed there.

For in the distance, far back into the depths of the Borderland, a blue glow was forming. Just a pinprick of turquoise at first, but growing. Brighter and brighter all the time. Bigger and bigger. Nearer and nearer. The glow was rippling. A brilliant electric blue, it was, and swarming, like the thousands of stinging gnats that preyed on Freelanders all year round.

No, not gnats. But people. Real live people! Glowing brilliantly blue. They were nearer now, and KC could see. They were soldiers. Line upon line of them, row upon row, all marching in time with the non-existent beat of a non-existent drum coming from a non-existent band leader. Left. Right. Left. Right. Nearer. Nearer. The chink of their armour. KC could see now that it was their armour that was blue. The armour was glowing, light shining from it so that he could see clearly each breastplate that clanked up and down in time with the soldiers' marching. And the rifles. The glowing blue rifles, hitched high on the shoulder of each soldier's right arm. They were bigger than any rifle that any Freelander had ever owned. Twice the size! Three times! They must have been six feet, almost as tall as most of the soldiers themselves, those rifles. And they must hold at least twice as much ammunition as a normal rifle.

KC was stunned. It was the invasion. It was here at last, and KC had been the one who had spotted it. But KC had no time to praise himself for his efforts. He was up like a flash, sprinting as fast as he could towards the Domes. He forgot about his lunch bag back in the ditch, for now he was on automatic pilot. He'd run through this moment over and over again in his mind during the past two weeks, but now that it was finally here, now that it had arrived, KC didn't need to think. He just ran. He ran and he ran and he ran.

The journey, which usually took him about 15 minutes, KC managed in less than five. But the army was gaining. The giant blue army was behind him.

They were near the Border already. They were going twice the speed of KC. KC was spent, but at the sight of the blue army behind him, he put on a last spurt of speed, summoned from where he didn't know.

He hurtled into the Primary Dome. The President's Dome. Where he'd been told to come when this occasion arose.

"President Bellmore! President Bellmore! The army, they've arrived!" he screamed at the top of his voice, to the lobby at large. Suddenly the lobby was in uproar. People were rushing around, pushing him from side to side.

"They're here! The Borderlanders! They've come! The invaders have arrived!"

KC's mind was fuzzy. He was exhausted from the run and felt close to collapsing. But no one was paying him the slightest bit of attention. Parents were looking for children. The Vice-President was clearing an aisle for President Bellmore to come through. People were collecting together anything they could use as a weapon against the blue army: chair legs, silver candlesticks from the President's dining room, school girls' hockey sticks, kitchen knives, and the occasional ornamental shotgun or dagger.

But KC had seen the immensity of the army. He knew that they'd never stand a chance. The army was vast, disciplined and armed with weapons that the Freelanders had never before set their eyes upon. The Freelanders were doomed before they'd even begun.

In a terrified daze, KC went back out into the open. Outside, the air was filled with screams of frightened children and the thud of running heavy boots.

He strained his ears to hear the distant chink of blue armour. He couldn't yet hear it. Well at least that was something. With his head slightly clearing at this relatively promising prospect, KC ran through the Main Courtyard into the Secondary Dome. He needed to find his mother.

It was quite as hectic in this Dome as it had been in the Primary one. Fully grown men were running around in a panic, brandishing kitchen knives or cricket bats. KC squeezed through the masses of people, through the corridors, to his own, private area of the Dome. He burst into his living area.

"Mother, Mother, Mother! They're here, the Borderlanders, they're here!"

Karin was sitting in an armchair by the fire, wringing her hands nervously and looking through the transparent wall into the Courtyard at all the frantic bustling going on. She turned when KC entered, leapt up, and flung her arms around her son.

"Keitaro! You're alright!" she exclaimed, close to tears, her head buried in KC's shoulder. He was a head taller than Karin, as he'd had a growth spurt when he turned 14.

"It's KC," said KC, though without the fierceness that his voice usually had. He hadn't the heart to keep it up. He was too relieved to see her.

"Yes, yes, KC. Sorry. I'm just so relieved. It was you that spotted them, wasn't it? It was your shift."

KC nodded. "Yes. Yes, it was me. I saw them coming. Mother, they're so fierce! They have heavy blue armour and massive rifles! At least twice the size of our ones!"

44

"Oh, my! And it was my little Keitaro, too! All on his own!"

KC stepped out of the embrace. "Mother, don't be stupid! I'm not to be praised! You should be scared. Really scared. We won't have a chance. Mother, I've seen them."

"Yes, KC, you're right, of course. We should leave. Now."

KC nodded. "Yes, I don't want to fight. It will be a massacre. We'll be killed instantly."

"We must pack, quickly. Where's your lunch bag, KC? We can use that, it had food in it already," said Karin.

"No, Mother. I left it at the Border. I forgot about it, sorry. But really, we don't have time. They're on their way alrea–"

But KC was cut off. There was a loud crash, right outside the Dome. KC spun around and though the glassy metallic sheeting he could see blue. Wave upon wave of blue soldiers marched past the Dome. They were here at last.

KC scanned the Courtyard to find out where the crash had come from. With horror he saw that the Primary Dome was a Dome no more. The metallic sheeting had shattered and tiny splinters of glass-like metal were whizzing around in the air. They were whirling round in mini-twisters, ebbing and flowing. In some places they were going at 100 miles an hour. Enough to embed in his skull quite nicely – and most probably come out the other side. There was only another thin sheet of transparent metal – much the same as the shattered one – separating KC and

Karin from this monster.

The blue army was still coming. The occasional soldier would fall at the hands of a cricket bat or kitchen knife brandished by the bravest Freelanders, but on the whole they were untouched, and they just kept coming. Very few stopped to fight.

But one did.

KC had only enough time to register what was about to happen. One blue-armoured soldier stopped. He lost his place in the ranks, but the rest just marched around him. The soldier turned around until he was looking directly at KC. He raised his rifle and looked down the barrel. Right through the Dome wall and into KC's chest. KC took in the puckered bluish-grey cheeks and scrawny chin and neck. His glowing blue helmet covered the top half of his head but his eyes were visible between the eye-slits. The eyes were slits themselves – blood-red and showing no emotion, only the red of cold-blooded murder.

KC had a split second to react. He didn't even have enough time to shout out any warning to Karin. He leapt backwards, cannoning into her. She was knocked to the ground and he landed on top. She screamed as an electric blue bullet collided with the metal of the Dome. The Dome shattered, but the bullet kept going. It whistled past KC's head, an inch from his ear – where his heart had been just a moment before.

He didn't dare get up. The metallic shards that had a second ago made up the giant Secondary Dome structure were now mingling with the shards of the Primary Dome. All were whizzing around above his head in a deadly hail. Below him, he felt Karin move, try to get up.

"No, Mother! Don't!"

But Karin was stronger than she looked. She didn't seem to realize the danger that she'd put both herself and KC in if she got up. She forced KC to roll off her and onto the floor beside her. She got gingerly to her knees...

"NO!" shouted KC.

He saw it all, as if in slow motion. The splinter of metal swooping low to the ground at nearly 100 miles per hour. Karin's head coming to meet it. KC lunged forward, trying to knock Karin back down so that her head would miss the speeding shard of metal. He was a fraction of a second too late. He watched, paralyzed, as the metal shard collided with Karin's head. Her skull was punctured, and blood pumped out. Karin fell backward, her eyes glassy and her body stiff.

KC looked away. He knew she was dead. He couldn't cry. He was too defeated. He threw himself to the ground. She was dead. She was dead, and it was all his fault. The blue army was slaughtering the Freelanders, and his world was over. All three Freeland Domes were flattened. The thunder of the boots on earth was fading... The clang of armour was lessening... His horizontal view was growing dim...

But he could vaguely sense a hand on his shoulder and he thought he could hear the distant murmuring of a man's voice. It was only just above him, but it felt miles away – in another world, almost.

"Come, son. I'm here. To take you somewhere safe."
KC fainted.

******

KC sat bolt upright in bed. It was dark. Sweat was pouring down his forehead, but he was shivering from the cold. He pulled the thin white blanket that covered him up to his chin, and peered owlishly over the top. It was the same dream every night. The same blue sky, the same glassy Domes, and the same glowing blue army. The images were clear now, but soon they would fade and KC would be left with nothing but the blueness of the sky. The blueness of the sky that never, ever left him.

KC closed his eyes again and slipped back into sleep. But this was a peaceful, dreamless sleep of nothing but the soothing darkness.

******

When KC next awoke, it was to the hustle and bustle of late morning. People were up and about around him, and he knew he'd slept in. He blinked in the light and rubbed his eyes. He sat up in bed, and the nurse approached.

"Ah, Keitaro. You're awake," she smiled.

"It's KC," KC said stonily back.

"KC, of course, of course. So, KC. How are you feeling?"

"Okay," he lied. He had a headache and he was dreadfully thirsty. But he thought it best not to say anything.

"Good, good. Well, KC, you have a visitor," the nurse said, still smiling her fixed smile. KC straightened up.

"A visitor? No, there must be some mistake. I never get visitors... I don't have a family."

"That's not quite true, KC." He was about to ask her what she meant by that, but she retreated down the ward. In her place stood a tall, skinny man with a long, once-handsome face, and deep, soulful green eyes. His dark, shiny hair had streaks of silver in it, betraying his age. He had on a long, dark cloak that was billowing around his ankles even though there was no wind in the ward. It was eerie.

"Er, hallo," said KC, not really sure how to greet this stranger. "How did you get here? I never saw you come." The stranger laughed. It was a warm, friendly laugh, but KC would have been more comfortable had he known what the stranger was laughing at.

"Oh, the same way as everyone else, son. But I dare say I can be discreet when I want to."

KC didn't know what to say to this. He opened his mouth, and then shut it again.

"I came to see if you were okay," said the stranger. "Last time I saw you, you were in a very bad way."

"Well, thank you," said KC, taken aback. "I hadn't expected any visitors..."

"No," laughed the man, humourlessly. "I don't expect you had. But you have me."

There was silence. KC was the one to break it.

"I'm sorry sir, but I still don't really know who you are," he said, nervously.

"True, true. I haven't really introduced myself..."

He paused, as if at a loss of what to say. "Dear, dear, this is hard. Mind if I sit down, boy?"

KC shook his head. "I don't mind," he said, not seeing where there was for the man to sit down.

"Thank you. My name is Ike." He perched on the edge of KC's bed. KC tucked his legs up, hurriedly.

"Ike," said KC, as if this introduction wasn't good enough.

"Just Ike," Ike said. Then fell silent again.

"Pleased to meet you, Just Ike," replied KC, beginning to feel uncomfortable. "My name is KC."

Ike laughed. "Pleased to see you still have a sense of humour, lad. After all you've been through. It's important, that is."

"What do you mean, after all I've been through?" asked KC, suspiciously.

A frown creased across Ike's brow. "Well, after the Blue Army invaded. You know, lad, you were the only survivor," said Ike, bordering on incredulity.

KC shook his head sadly. "I don't remember the day," he explained.

"Oh." Ike's face darkened. "I see."

"Why, should I?"

Ike shrugged. "No, not especially. I mean to say, I can see why you wouldn't. It was a terrible day. But it makes my job a whole lot harder."

"What exactly is your job?" asked KC.

"KC, don't you recognize me? At all?"

KC shook his head. "I've told you. I don't remember that day. Or much before it, for that matter. I remember the blue sky. And I remember Karin – that's my mother by the way – and the Freeland Domes,

50

I think. You aren't a Freelander, are you? You said yourself that I was the only survivor..."

Ike looked away, sadly, and sniffed. "No. I was. But I'm not now. I was thrown out when – when – er, 14 years ago."

KC took in this piece of information, filing it away, but deciding not to pursue it. He could tell it upset Ike.

"So why are you here?" KC asked, changing the subject hastily. This was obviously a touchy subject.

"To take you somewhere safe."

KC was halfway through opening his mouth to ask another question, when he stopped. He'd heard that somewhere before. That voice. That same deep, gruff voice. And slowly, ever so slowly, his memories began to return...

... a swarming mass of tiny blue specks... a pair of red slits peering through an electric blue helmet... a speeding bullet coming straight to him from the barrel of a six-foot rifle... a million deadly shards of metal, swirling around above his head... the staring, glassy, ice-blue eyes of his mother as she fell back... a hand on his shoulder and the gentle words, "To take you somewhere safe."

"It was you," said KC, snapping back to the present and looking into Ike's eyes. "Wasn't it?"

Ike looked confused. "What was me, lad?"

"It was you, you were there. You saved my life, didn't you?"

Ike nodded, sincerely. "Yes, son. That was me. I brought you here. Just temporarily, you understand. Just until I could find somewhere safer. For good."

"But why? Why me? There must have been loads of others that you could have helped. I mean, you must be as powerful as the Borderlanders if you were able to get me, even to get yourself, out of there alive." It all came out in a rush. Why had he been saved? Why not President Bellmore? The President was more important. So why him? And how, for that matter? This man was powerful, that much was obvious. Powerful enough to save a 14-year-old boy from certain death.

"I'd just be grateful you're alive, sonny boy."

"I'd rather be dead," said KC, bluntly. The stupid man didn't understand a thing, he thought.

Ike's face blackened and he suddenly gripped KC's shoulders with surprising force. "You don't mean that, KC. You don't mean that. Don't ever say that," he said fiercely, shaking KC.

"Well it's true!" spat KC. "How do you think I feel? All my family gone. I've no one left. You hear me? No one. I'd rather die."

Ike let go of KC, who sank back on his pillows. "That isn't true, KC."

"Oh yeah?" replied KC bitterly.

"Yes, son."

There was a pause, in which Ike looked thoughtful and KC looked stormy, refusing to look at Ike. Eventually Ike spoke.

"You have me."

"Yeah, you. A guy I've only met once, and didn't even remember meeting until a minute ago."

There was another uncomfortable pause, but eventually Ike gulped and lifted KC's chin so that

KC had no choice but to look at him. KC struggled, but Ike held firm.

"Keitaro Michelangelo Claudius Brown. I'm your father."

KC's jaw tried to drop, but Ike was still holding it, so it couldn't. He looked at Ike properly. Now he could see the likeness. They had the same emerald green eyes and thick dark lashes, the same sleek dark hair – but, mercifully, his without the grey – and the same long, thin face. He couldn't think what to say, so he said what he always said when anyone addressed him as Keitaro.

"It's KC."

KC's father laughed. "Yes, of course it is. What was Karin thinking when she named you?"

KC joined in the laughter. It was the first time he'd laughed since Blue Sky Day, and he'd forgotten how much he enjoyed the experience.

"I don't know. But I wouldn't have it any other way. My name is Keitaro Michelangelo Claudius Brown. But it's KC to you."

The End

David Wood

David Wood wrote his first play for children in 1967 and has since written over 50 more. They are performed all over the world, and include *The Gingerbread Man*, *The Selfish Shellfish*, and six adaptations of Roald Dahl's work including *The BFG* and *The Witches*. He has been awarded an OBE and has received several playwriting awards. David is also a children's author, a performer and a magician!

Steph Sewell

Steph is 11 and lives in Bristol. Her favourite Blue Peter pet is Shelley the tortoise because she reminds her of her Dad, slow and dopey-looking! Steph enjoys reading Darren Shan, JK Rowling and Terry Pratchett. In her spare time she loves eating chocolate, watching football and spending money. Of writing *Sam's Spider*, she said, "The thing I enjoyed most was making my story funny!"

Sam's Spider

Steph Sewell and David Wood

CAST:

Sam   8 years old
Carly 12 years old, Sam's sister.
Spider (very brief but extremely important
             appearance)

SET:

Sam's bedroom – bed, window, open door,
bedside table and lamp (on), clothes on chair,
books and toys on windowsill.

[Enter SAM, wearing pyjamas and carefully carrying a glass of water in one hand, a comic in the other. As he comes through the open door it slowly and mysteriously starts to close behind him. Then CARLY, in jeans and t-shirt, pops out from behind it.]

CARLY: Boo!

SAM *[Jumping]*: Ah!

[He nearly spills his water. CARLY laughs.]

[Realizing] Carly! Don't do that!

> *[CARLY tickles him.]*

No! Stop it!

> *[But he can't help laughing.]*

CARLY: Night, Sam.

SAM: Night.

> *[CARLY exits.]*

> *[SAM puts the comic on the bed, puts the glass of water on the bedside table, then folds back the duvet to get into bed. Suddenly and piercingly...]*

Aaaaah!

> *[He jumps back in surprise, staring at the bed.]*

> *[CARLY enters at speed.]*

CARLY: What is it?

SAM *[Pointing]*: S – s – spider! In my bed! *[Sudden thought]* You put it there!

CARLY: I didn't!

SAM: Did!

CARLY: Didn't!

[She pushes SAM towards the bed.]

SAM: No!

CARLY *[In a childish voice]*: Doesn't lickle brother like spiders?

SAM: Not much.

CARLY: Get rid of it then.

SAM: How?

CARLY: Bash it!

> *[She picks up the comic, rolls it up, and starts hitting the bed.]*

Kapow! Zap!

SAM: No! Carly, don't kill it!

CARLY: Why not? It's only a spider! And lickle Sam doesn't like spiders!

> *[She hits the bed again.]*

Exterminate!

SAM: Stop it! It doesn't deserve to die. It may be lost. Maybe its big sister's out looking for it.

CARLY: Oh yes? If you were lost, do you think I'd come looking for you?

SAM: I hope you would.

CARLY: No way! *[Cheerfully]* Night, Sam!

[She throws the comic on the bed and flounces out, pulling the door to behind her.]

SAM: But, Carly...

[He thinks for a moment. He checks the spider is still there. He decides to be brave and humanely remove it. He opens the window, then drinks the water from the glass. He carefully approaches the spider.]

Don't move, spider. Please. I'm not going to hurt you.

[He takes the comic and slides it under the spider, then puts the glass over it. He carefully takes it to the window.]

Off you go. Find your big sister! Night!

[He gently shakes it out of the window, then pulls the window to.]

[He puts down the glass, gets into bed and looks at his comic.]

[Close-up of alarm clock at 20:40. The clock ticks. SAM drops asleep. The comic falls from his fingers.]

[Close-up of alarm clock at midnight. The clock ticks.]

[The room is darker, though the bedside light is still on.]

[Sudden noises, spooky clunks. Scratching and breathing.]

[SAM wakes up. He listens. Then, warily, he looks at the window. The window opens eerily and a thick, furry, probing, giant spider's leg appears, getting longer and longer as it slowly but surely enters the room...]

[SAM watches wide-eyed.]

[Fade out.]

******

End of David's section. Steph continues...

******

[One, two, three legs, another one, a body, then four more legs slip into the room.]

[The humungous SPIDER turns round and directs eight large, yellow eyes at sam.]

[SAM turns completely white and nearly faints.]

SPIDER: You've squished my Charles, haven't you?

[SAM opens and closes his mouth like a goldfish but says nothing.]

SPIDER: That was the three thousand, two hundred and fifty-sixth Charles I've lost this year.

I mean, do you know how painful it is to give birth to all those babies?

[SAM shakes his head and the faintest hint of a smile appears at the corner of his mouth.]

[The SPIDER detects this and beams back, revealing two long, razor-sharp fangs.]

[SAM goes rigid again.]

SAM: Are you going to eat me?

SPIDER: Heavens, no! Why would I do that?

SAM: 'Cause, 'cause you're big and scary and big. And I thought that that was what giant, talking spiders do?

SPIDER: Goodness, what have you been reading? Humans squish my babies all the time, so there isn't really much point me getting upset about it.

SAM: But I didn't squish your baby, I let him go.

SPIDER: My ickle Charlie is still alive?

SAM: Yes!

SPIDER: Oh, thank you so much! Is there anything I can do to repay you?

SAM *[With an evil grin]*: Well, now you mention it, there is one thing you can do for me.

[A moment later, from CARLY'S bedroom...]

CARLY: Aaaaauuaaaaaaaaaaaaah!!

The End

Raymond Briggs

Raymond Briggs is one of the most successful picture book creators of all time, and has won the prestigious Kate Greenaway Medal twice. He has written and illustrated classic children's books such as *The Snowman*, *Father Christmas* and *Fungus the Bogeyman*. These books have sold millions of copies worldwide. Raymond was awarded a gold Blue Peter badge in November 2004 for his contribution to children's literature.

Grace Owens

Grace is 13 and lives in Yorkshire with her three sisters, and their dog Esther. Of writing and illustrating *Time Knights*, she said, "Blending my style with Raymond Briggs' was difficult until I drew the illustrations, as this made writing the story easier, as I got a sense for the characters. My Daddy would have loved to have read this story, as he helped me write many previous stories, but unfortunately he died on Tuesday 11th October 2005."

The Time Knights

Grace Owens and Raymond Briggs

*Every evening, the old man, out walking his dog, paused
by the great hollow in the hill and gazed down into it. What
were they doing down there? Those children... they seemed
to be building something. What was it? Every day it grew
bigger, taller, wider. What on earth could it be?*

*"Wish my eyes were better," thought the old man. But
maybe they weren't children at all. Maybe they were small
aliens who look like children. And what were those funny
little things running about? They weren't cats or dogs. Do
aliens have animals? Why do some of the children have
odd rounded heads? Are they wearing* Bob the Builder
helmets? Perhaps real Earth children are helping the aliens.

*"Oh no!" cried the old man. "They're coming up here!
They're going to get me! Come on, Kelpie – run!"*

But the dog, prone to being unreliable, misunderstood the instruction and went racing down the hill to meet the creatures; the old man, still holding onto the lead, was forced to follow. They ran down the steep hill's grassy slopes. The sight would have been quite humorous to an onlooker, but for the old man it was an incredibly painful experience. His bad leg and heavy breathing soon slowed him though, and, unable to keep up with Kelpie, he unwillingly let go of the lead. Collapsing onto the grass he cursed his old age and bitterly glared at his bad leg. The grass was dry and prickly and he was only managing short painful gasps in the place of breathing properly. Exhausted, he sat panting for a while, completely involved in his own thoughts.

Footsteps in front of him, too close for comfort, awoke him from his daze, and, not quite knowing what he was going to see, he slowly raised his head. The face in front of him was smiling, and, unsure whether this was a good or a bad thing, he tried to look at the whole picture in front of him.

Slowly his jaw dropped, his eyes grew wide, and his face suddenly became peaked and pale as he focussed on the figure before him. After a while he became aware of a quiet snuffling beside him. He glanced down and saw a black velvety creature sniffing blindly at his feet: it was a mole.

And, if it was possible, his jaw dropped even further.

To the old man it felt as if he had been sat in that position for hours, but in actual fact it had been a matter of minutes, and the figure in front of him had obviously had enough of being stared at and was ready to make the introductions. He reached to his head and politely took off his bowler hat, bending forward in a bow, and the old man could see he did indeed have childish features.

He was quite short, but sturdily built, with stocky legs and a wide oval face; he had rosy cheeks and a cheeky grin. He was wearing a shirt, khaki green in colour with dark green buttons, his shorts were brown and loose, and he was wearing a thick pair of boots worn with muddy white ankle socks.

Altogether the outfit looked quite old-fashioned, but the little man seemed quite unaware of his strange appearance as he began to speak:

"Come to see you have we,
Built our shelter secretly,
Brought you here mysteriously,
My friends and me."

Whatever the old man had been expecting, it wasn't this. He was quite at a loss as to what to say. They seemed friendly enough – or at least this one did – but could it be an act?

"W-what?"

"Have we surprised you?
We did not know what to do,
We dressed like you used to,
In order not to scare you."

The little man seemed so upset that the old man tried to say something sounding less shocked. But looking at the little man and his friends, he could see the outfit was somewhat familiar, something he might have worn once. How would they know this? Just one of them wearing it would have been bad enough, but with them all in identical suits it was rather daunting. So what he meant to sound polite and conversational came out in a high-pitched panicky voice, and his idea to be calm and rational went down the drain.

"Who are you? How do you know me?"

"We are the Time Knights,
Keeping history to rights.
We have seen many sights,
And know more people than our knights."

What did that mean? His head was spinning with rhymes.

"But why have you come to see me?" The old man was getting more confused by their explanations, and his head was still thumping from his run.

"We have something to show,
But we soon have to go,
So come and we'll tell you what we know.
Look into the mirror and see what it will show."

"And the moles?"

"They are our friends,
They help us with our history mends.
But come now before it's too late,
And we have to leave your future to fate."

The old man felt himself being gently pulled to his feet, and, completely forgetting his earlier suspicions and going against his better judgement, he followed them down the hill.

They led him down the hill. The evening air was cold on his neck, the breeze tickled his hair, and his boots padded softly in the damp grass; but, unaware of his surroundings, the old man wondered anxiously what they were going to show him. His thick anorak flapped in the wind and he shoved his hands into his pockets to try and keep them warm. Dusk was falling, and he watched the sky as it threw a pinky glow over the hills. The air was cold on his teeth, and his cheeks and his eyes watered where the wind cut sharply across his face. All along his path were molehills, little mountains of soil. He would have stood on them if the little men in front hadn't so pointedly avoided them and, not wanting to offend them, he politely did the same.

He had never been down this part of the hill. It was strange. He did not feel like himself; he was a grumpy old man who didn't like anybody's company but his own and Kelpie's, yet here he was doing the most ridiculous thing he had ever done, walking with strange children who talked in rhyme and called themselves 'Time Knights'. He stared ahead, trying to get a clearer view of where they were taking him, but his eyes were weak at the best of times – never mind when they were full of salty tears. But after walking several hundred yards he gradually built up a picture of the shelter that he had seen being built, and as he turned to look at it he was taken by surprise yet again.

The shelter seemed incredibly small, just tall enough to take his height of six foot three; but the entrance was so low he had to bow down fully to get in. Around the entrance little black faces kept appearing, and then disappearing under the floor of the shelter. The shelter was  made of sticks neatly woven together, almost like a hut. Moss filled the gaps, mud was crusted round the arch that served as an entrance, and leaves blew out through the door, but what struck him most was how unnoticeable it was. He wondered how he could have possibly seen it so well from above.

Inside, it smelt sweetly musty and damp. He glanced around, but there wasn't much to see. The ground was carpeted with a fresh layer of leaves, which were dancing in circles beneath his feet, and on the back wall there was a mirror. It was arched, with a bland wooden frame, the glass was chipped and rusty around the edges, and though it looked nondescript and had an unassuming air about it, it stood proudly in its place, staring blankly back at the room. He stared into it, but no face stared back out at him, it stayed empty – but before he could think this through, the little man came in behind him and started another of his poems.

"The mirror tells its secrets when it chooses,
Force them from it and it refuses,
It remembers things you won't,
Memories sad and happy things you don't."

So he stared at the mirror, waiting, not knowing what to expect and not even knowing why he was there anyway. The mirror stayed blank, and when his frustration was nearly at its limit, suddenly an image grew behind the glass. A girl stared back at him, smiling. He remembered her: Mary Dingle, the girl he had met in the 1940s when he was evacuated. She seemed prettier than he remembered, wearing her

school clothes, a satchel resting on her hip, and holding onto the strap just like he remembered. She had been his best friend.

He had been so lonely when he had been sent away, he had had no friends – they had all laughed at his London accent, tripped him up and made faces at him. He had met Mary Dingle walking home after a miserable day at school; she had looked just like the mirror image in front of him now. He and her had got on so well, they had spent an enjoyable hour spitting cherry pips at passers-by from up a tree. After that, they had walked home together every night, getting up to other mischievous antics.

The mirror changed and there she and his younger self stood, looking out at him. She had been his first girlfriend, and they had been inseparable, always laughing and joking together. They had often gone round the neighbourhood stealing cooling

buns off the window sills; they had played in the fields collecting conkers in the autumn and daisies in the summer. It was John and Mary, Mary and John, and often it had merged into one – JohnandMary. It became a saying in the village: "Don't worry, one day you'll be a JohnandMary."

The scene changed, and now there was no one in the mirror, but a tree with 'MD' and 'JT' engraved upon its trunk was there instead. He remembered the day they went there. The sun had been scorching, and her mother had packed a picnic for them both. Mary had spent the whole time trying to find the perfect spot. "Just a little further" meant another half a mile, and by the time she had found it they

had walked five miles; but even he had had to admit that the tree was beautiful and the dancing shadows it cast were so refreshing. They had eaten cold sausages and chicken legs for lunch, made all the more special because her mother

71

had saved them carefully, as meat was hard to come by, even in the countryside, because of rationing.

Then the mirror went blank again, and this time nothing else appeared. The old man, John, still stared intently as if looking for something else. He was actually remembering what had happened after that. They had promised always to keep in touch, and when he had been sent home at the end of the war he had waited expectantly for her letter. She had promised  to write first, but no letter came. Day after day he had waited on the step looking into the busy London streets, wishing to see fields of green. After weeks he finally gave up, but every time the doorbell rang he had still turned round expecting to see Mary. He heard her talking to him when the room was empty, and he laughed at his own jokes expecting to hear her merry chuckle too.

He had moved from London when he was grown-up, out to the countryside, and become more and more solitary. Apart from Kelpie he had no friends.

 He looked around him, but the shelter was empty, and only the whistling of the wind could be heard. The little man was gone, but there in his place was a letter. He stared at it.

His name was written in round, childish handwriting along with his old London address, and stamped across the front were the words 'LOST POST-WAR MAIL'.

Here was the letter he had never received.

******

He waited, looking at the door of Mary's old house. It stood ajar, and a sliver of light shone on the step. Not sure what to do, he shifted from foot to foot gripping the open letter in his sweaty hand, wondering whether or not it was even likely that Mary still lived here. He nervously peeked through the door. He jumped as he heard a familiar voice from inside.

"Come in dear, the door's open, don't stand there with a mouth like a fish's!"

He opened the door fully and came into a passage; he turned left, into the sitting room, and even as he walked in he could tell that nothing had changed. And there Mary sat, doing her knitting. She had more wrinkles than he remembered, and her chestnut hair was greying and changed from pigtails to a bun, but she stared up at him with the same twinkling blue eyes and mischievous smile, and said, in the same blunt voice:

"Where've you been? I've been waiting for you for 60-odd years!"

The End

Anthony Horowitz

Anthony Horowitz's popular Alex Rider books, about the adventures of a 14-year-old spy for Britain's MI6, have seen him win a number of literary awards. *Skeleton Key* won the 2003 Red House Children's Book Award, and *Stormbreaker* was shortlisted for the same award in 2000, as was *Point Blanc* in 2001. The first Alex Rider book, *Stormbreaker*, is currently being made into a film. Anthony's latest Alex Rider book, *Ark Angel*, is out now, as is *Raven's Gate*, the first book in his new Power of Five series.

Tom Hindson

Tom is 13 years old and lives in Essex with his sisters. He enjoys reading Anthony Horowitz, JRR Tolkien and Eoin Colfer. In his spare time he's a supporter of Middlesborough football team. Of writing *Natives!*, he said, "I enjoyed thinking up an exciting plot to follow on from the opening paragraph. The hardest part was thinking of a really good ending."

Natives!

Tom Hindson and Anthony Horowitz

The snake was a fer-de-lance. I recognised it instantly from the brown, speckled markings and its length – this one was about two metres – and from the sheer ugliness of its eyes. Quickly, I tried to remember as much about it as I could. The fer-de-lance was a type of pit viper. It was the most dangerous snake in South America. When it struck, it would move so fast it would become a blur. It normally injected its target with about 105mg of deadly venom. 50mg was enough to kill an adult and I would need slightly less because I was only 13 years old. The snake was in my shower. That was the bad news. But the worse news was, so was I…

I had to move quickly, but too fast and the deadly snake would attack. I slowly grabbed the showerhead and turned it onto full heat, spraying it around the cubicle as slowly and evenly as possible, confusing the snake by heating up the walls and floor. Because the snake could only see heat, I hoped it would not be able to see me properly.

It worked; the viper lifted its head ready to pounce. Now all I had to do was to make sure it wasn't pouncing at me. It pounced. I jumped. Too late. It caught my leg, just above my ankle. I examined the wound and saw it was not the deep puncture wound that it should be but a long gash, just across the surface of my skin, barely deep enough to draw blood, harmless.

I had escaped, just.

Two days later we were packing up to go on a 15-kilometre trek through the Amazon jungle to another village. The first experience hadn't been great. On the first night a giant snake had been planted in my shower by the natives, and on the second they had come and looted anything they could, setting fire to one of the huts and killing someone. Mum said that they were jealous of all the things we had but I think it was the fact that for the past 50 years, civilisation had been cutting down the only world that the native tribes know, the rainforest. They could do nothing as bulldozers rolled in and destroyed everything that they had. Now they were getting their own back, however they could. In the weeks before we left for Brazil there had been reports of violence and hostility by the Amazonian tribes but, as ever, Mum ignored them and we were here.

"Right, everyone ready? We're leaving," she proclaimed. She was like that. Always doing what she thought was best, no matter what anyone else said. When she was told she was a stone overweight, she said that maybe the scales were a stone underweight. She wouldn't pay the higher congestion charge price for a 4X4; she said that the mayor was jealous because he couldn't afford a 4X4. She was told pollution creates a hole in the atmosphere, so she wrote a letter to the Prime Minister asking him to mend it. It was annoying but I had grown used to it.

So we started our trip across 15 kilometres of humid rainforest. Mum had said that we would do five kilometres at a time, but she didn't think that there would be swamps and hills and bushes and mosquitoes. So after six hours, five stops and three kilometres covered she finally gave into the idea that we might be camping that night.

"Set your tent up, Matthew," she ordered. "And John, set up mine and yours, we'll be camping here tonight."

Dad and I duly set to it while Mum 'supervised'. I don't know why but I never felt easy putting that tent up, I felt like someone was watching me. At the time I told myself that it was Mum staring at me. But it felt like the staring was coming from behind me. Dad obviously felt it too, as he kept glancing round, looking worried.

As we ate that night I definitely saw a pair of deep brown eyes poking through the trees, but when I went to investigate I found nothing. However, later that night I woke up to the sound of shuffling feet and after a few seconds was rather surprised to be staring at my arm, which had a trickle of blood running down it, and a 15-inch rock point attached to a four-foot wood pole with a native on the other end.

I initiated a staring contest with him, giving me time to find out what was happening. (I was extremely good at staring contests, and in school they had often freaked my teachers out so much that I had been let off detentions.) I saw that the man, if you could call him that, was very young, naked but for a bum-flap, and covered in paint. His spear also had a large, round rock on the other end.

Idiot. I grabbed the pole and swung it across his head, knocking him unconscious. I jumped up and saw three other people around Mum and Dad's tents, and two more coming towards me. I jumped and dodged their spear attacks, but they were older and more experienced than the one lying on the ground. I had to run. I knew it was cowardice and that I was deserting my parents but I was their only chance. Mum would think up an escape plan that was totally mad and wouldn't even be considered by a three-year-old, and Dad would be forced into attempting it. They would get killed. So, with tears in my eyes, I grabbed my bag, turned and ran away from the natives and my parents. It was the hardest thing that I have done or ever will do in my life, but I did it.

I followed the tribe through the night at a distance, keeping well out of sight of any of them, and of Mum and Dad. If I was seen by any of them then I would be lying on the ground in more than one piece, to put it nicely. They took Mum and Dad to a village with about 30 small huts and a massive statue. I mean, HUGE. It was twice the size of the trees and was just one column: a totem pole with hundreds of heads on it. The main one was about ten feet up and had a picture of a monkey god on it, with two spikes hanging out the sides of his head. As I walked round, I saw that there were also spikes right down the back of the pole, like a ladder.

Mum and Dad had been taken to the biggest hut;

it was a 20-foot circle with an upside-down ice cream cone made of thatch on top. Although it was better made than the rest, it had plenty of gaps in the wall that I could peek through to see what was going on. Mum and Dad were tied to two stumps and the head tribesman (you could tell he was in charge by the assortment of bird feathers in his hair) uttered chants and danced around. He then got a small knife and cut Mum and Dad in very precise places, not deeply or anywhere near vital organs, but he drew blood, which another tribesman collected and drank, before passing the bowl round to the others in the hut. I found this disgusting. I had to go out into the forest and was sick.

When I returned, Mum and Dad were not in the hut but lying on the floor in front of the totem pole. They had been decorated with leaves and paint and were obviously going to be sacrifices. I guessed the ceremony would start at sunrise. I looked at my watch: four o'clock. I probably had two hours.

I left the village and, in the forest, emptied the contents of my bag: two torches, some deodorant, a book, a few nuts (brazil, cashew), my MP3 player, my phone and some matches, and the bag itself.

At five I crept round the back of the camp to where the totem pole was, to prepare my rescue. I had discarded the nuts and my MP3, which were now floating down the Amazon in a bag, but I had kept the deodorant, book, torches and matches. They were part of my plan.

The natives had already started when I got back (I obviously didn't know as much as I thought about

Amazonian native rituals), the head tribesman leading the rest of the villagers in a mass. They were all on their hands and knees, noses on the ground, still as statues, gently humming. I waited as long as I could, but I wanted to make my escape before dawn, so at half five I climbed up the back of the totem pole with all my equipment, to the main god. There was, as I had seen, holes in place of his mouth and eyes. I tore out some of the book pages and sprayed them with deodorant. When I had ripped out all the pages of the book I grabbed my torches and stuffed them into the eye sockets. Then I took a match and lit it, grabbed the deodorant and sprayed the match.

It worked perfectly. The line of fire sprayed out of the mouth, setting the scrunched-up pages alight. They then flew out of the mouth like fireballs. I also turned on the torches, lighting up the eyes. All of the natives looked up, but not many had seen the fire. I had prepared for that. I had only sent out some of the pages, the rest were being stuffed frantically in the mouth, ready for another burning. This time everyone saw the flames and most of the tribe just collapsed with fear. I called to Mum and Dad telling them I was round the back. They came round but as I turned to jump down I caught my shirt on one of the spikes. When they saw me Mum called out, "We knew you were coming, what are you doing up there?"

"Just hanging around," I replied.

I jumped down and was just walking into the woods when a spear flew through the air past my head and into a nearby tree. I turned around and there were about ten natives, nine armed with spears. Somehow I knew they weren't inviting us back for tea.

"Run, get to the river," I screamed at Mum and Dad. They didn't hang around. I guess even Mum realised that I was in charge and for once even she was not going to argue. I grabbed the spear from the tree and ran after Mum and Dad.

We got to the river where there were three open canoes and oars lying on the banks. Dad was already lowering one canoe onto the water and Mum was attempting to sabotage the other ones with a cup, dipping it into the water and tipping it into the boats. I grabbed some oars and jumped in, followed by Dad and, finally, Mum. At the last minute I grabbed the spear and put it into the boat.

"Paddle like mad downstream," I said.

"Er, Matt," Dad whispered. "Company!" The natives were already in the boats.

"Faster!" I paddled like mad for about ten minutes, sweat pouring down my face, my arms and back burning. Dad was the same and Mum was doing her best. Eventually, one of the natives' boats caught up with us and was coming across to capsize our boat. I grabbed the spear and jammed it in their hull creating a massive hole. The boat slowed down and sank quite quickly.

One down, one to go. The second boat came up alongside us, but now we had no spear to throw at them. They threw things at us, most missed but one particularly sharp rock caught my cheek. Blood poured down my face and onto my clothes but I didn't stop paddling. Suddenly we went round a bend in the river and there was a waterfall dead ahead.

"What do we do?" screamed Dad.

"Jump out John, and swim, and Matt can carry me on his shoulders," suggested Mum.

"No!" I screamed "You couldn't swim, the water's too fast. Jam your oar on the right of the boat and don't move it."

They both did what I said. The canoe didn't move. 30 metres, 25... 20... 15... the canoe drew perilously close to the edge and then it started to turn, slowly at first, but it was turning. We got there with only a few metres to spare. We jumped out as our canoe went down the waterfall.

The other canoe fell too, but it had about ten natives in it. As it went over the edge, I saw the same deep brown eyes that had jammed the rock point in my arm, that the night before had been staring into mine. Suddenly all barriers of language, belief and race were gone, we were just two kids caught up in a fight neither of us had started. Then the eyes were gone.

Dead.

That was the only moment in the whole trip when I felt compassion for the natives, all the time before I had felt angry that they had taken my parents and about the fact that we couldn't just have a holiday in the forest – but, then, I felt sorry for them.

Two weeks later I was back at school, with a really cool scar on my face and the coolest story of how I got it. But, however many times I told the story, I always thought of the deep brown eyes staring at me as they went over the waterfall.

They didn't know there was a world out there, they didn't know about countries, politics or wars. All they wanted was to lead a simple life in the forest without the interruption of white men's bulldozers and money. We had taken that away from them.

The End

Malorie Blackman

Malorie Blackman has written over 50 books, including *Noughts and Crosses*, *Pig-Heart Boy*, *Hacker* and *Whizziwig*. She is also a scriptwriter and has written for programmes such as *Byker Grove*. Malorie has been awarded a number of literary prizes and a BAFTA for Best Children's Drama for CBBC's *Pig-Heart Boy*. Her latest book, which has taken her just over two years to write, is *Checkmate*.

Nina Landale

Nina is 14 and lives in Oxfordshire with her younger sister, a dog called Billy and two cats, Loretta and Enzo. Her favourite authors are Malorie Blackman, Louise Rennison and Cornelia Funke. Nina enjoys going to youth theatre and eating her mum's roast chicken. Of writing *Thoughts*, she said, "I enjoyed planning it and exploring the ideas I had. It was hard to edit it all at the end because I didn't want to get rid of any of my ideas."

Thoughts

Nina Landale and Malorie Blackman

Mind your own business. That's always been the major rule of my life. Not just a rule of thumb, but a rule of all my other fingers as well. Until, that is, I had my accident. There I was, walking home along the high street with Lee, chatting away and minding my own, when the next thing I knew, I was lying on the pavement with an express train roaring through my head. I struggled to open my eyes. Lee and a strange man wearing paint-splattered overalls were looking down at me anxiously.

"Are you okay?" the man asked. "I'm so sorry; the paint pot fell off my ladder and caught the side of your head. Thank god it was almost empty. I'm so sorry. Should I call an ambulance?"

"No. No, thanks." I struggled to my feet. I felt the side of my head. It was throbbing and I already had a lump the size of Venus there, but at least there was no blood. The express train took its time, but finally rumbled out of my brain. But then I realized something. Not gradually. Not in stages. It hit me all at once. As I looked at Lee and the strange man, I was aware of something amazing. Shocking. I could actually…

see a light coming off the top of their heads. It wasn't like a little light bulb or tiny patch of light. It was like a mane of glowing colours, not just yellows, but oranges, reds, purples. These lights were some of the most beautiful things I had ever seen, and it made me want to laugh and cry at the same time. I felt myself losing my thoughts as I stared at them.

But why was this happening? Was it really happening at all? Questions were flying round my brain like a swarm of bees, and I suddenly found myself so scared I could hardly breathe.

I looked over at Lee; she was watching me with a worried look. I could tell she was scared for me and I wanted so much to tell her that I was alright, but the truth was that I wasn't. She started to say something and at that moment all her thoughts, feelings, memories and ideas came flooding into my mind. Everything that Lee had ever eaten, said, thought or done was now flocking around my head like a stampede. I felt sick; there were personal thoughts in there. Things I never wanted to know – and yet I felt slightly intrigued.

I started sorting through her thoughts, always making sure I never went near the really personal ones, and yet it was almost as if they wanted me there. Some of them jumped out at me, willing me to explore them. I was out of my depth, and I knew it, but there was still this urge to find the answers to the questions I had always asked myself. Was I her best friend or not? Did she think I was a nerd like all the other kids did? Now I could know once and for all.

A thought jumped out at me, it concerned Lee's sadness at the deaths she had encountered in her life. This wasn't right, I decided suddenly. These were private memories. I should be sticking to my old rule of just minding my own business, it had always kept me out of trouble.

I withdrew from Lee's thoughts and tried to clear my head, but as soon as the thoughts went, my head was strangely quiet and empty. *Don't be stupid!* I told myself, calmly. *This is just a bad dream, and it will all end soon.*

This reassured me. I took two deep breaths. Lee was still standing there watching me, as if she was scared I had gone mad.

"What?" I asked her. She was getting on my nerves.

"Are you alright, Sam? You've gone all pale, and... your eyes are..." She trailed off. I probably was pale, but this was a dream, nothing more.

I started to walk away, and immediately I got a searing pain in my head. I gasped, and held my head in my hands; it was throbbing painfully.

Lee was beside me in seconds. "Sam, what's wrong?"

I didn't know what was wrong. You don't feel pain in dreams. I felt a tear trickling down my cheek. Not only were other people's thoughts invading my head, but I couldn't move without pain. I was probably brain-damaged, I thought desperately. *Don't think about that Sam!* I told myself. *You will be fine, just concentrate on going home.*

I looked at Lee, she had her mobile out. "I'm calling your mum, Sam," she said. That at least felt right. Lee (or Leanne, as the teachers call her) is my best mate in the whole world, she has always stood by me, always helped me through anything. When Dad died I was inconsolable, but she had stuck through my silences, my mood swings, even when I had told her to get lost, she had stayed, making it better. But now I felt distant from her. The week before she had arranged a surprise birthday party for me – I was 13 now, and happy about it.

I thought she'd ring the loony bin if she found out what was going on. I did the one thing I should never have done. I ran!

Through bursts of pain, through groups of people, I fled. Down the roads I knew, the streets I had walked along every day of my life, and yet now they felt different. My senses seemed more acute: through the blinding pain I could feel the stickiness of the tarmac, smell the pungent oils, and taste the bitter fumes of pollution. And somewhere, far away, I could hear Lee shouting after me!

******

I remember very little about that first night. Only staggering through the front door and racing upstairs to my room. I put my head under the pillow, and prayed for all I was worth that it would be gone in the morning. I know Mum came up and tried to speak to me, but I couldn't face her. If I got her thoughts in my head then there would be no safe place left. I couldn't bear that!

Lee came round and told my mum all about the accident. Mum came up again, and I ignored her, then my alarm was beeping.

I dressed in my school uniform. My thoughts

were all groggy, and I knew that something had happened, but I couldn't remember what. I made my way downstairs and into the kitchen. Mum was cooking me some porridge. She only did that when she wanted to have a serious 'chat'. *What about?* I wondered. Then, as I sat down, my head started throbbing again, and with that throb the whole thing came back. The paint pot, Lee, the thoughts, the manes of light. I felt sick and suddenly wanted to cry. I had to tell Mum, she'd know what to do.

"Mum..." I said shakily, "there is ummm... something I need to say..." I was half-whispering and she turned towards me, and then I realized that I hadn't heard her thoughts.

"Actually, you know what, never mind!" I said, smiling. It had all been a horrid dream, nothing more.

"What is it, Sam?" Mum asked, she too was smiling at me. She could sense that I was happy. I felt like throwing my arms around her. I looked up at her smiling face, and then it happened again. My head started filling with Mum's thoughts. Despair gripped me, and I started to shake. I looked away. I would have to live in the Sahara Desert, where no people were. That would be the only way to survive. It wasn't just the fact that I was hearing voices, but also that it hurt to have them there. They gave me such a headache.

Mum grabbed me by the shoulders and looked at me. "What is it, Samantha?" She had used my full name, and that meant she wanted answers. But once again her thoughts immediately entered my head and blocked out everything else. I looked away, and then I found salvation. The thoughts only entered my head when I looked at Mum.

Could I control this nightmare by controlling how much eye contact I had? I tried out my theory. Oh joy, I was right. If I looked my mum in the eyes, her thoughts would come rushing in. But if I looked away, the thoughts stayed in her head. I felt ecstatic. I had found a way to stay sane. I was the boss. As long as I didn't look anyone in the eye, nobody's thoughts would ever fill my mind again. Ever!

******

School. The place with the zero tolerance policy on bullying. The only place I get bullied. I hate it so much that when I hear the alarm in the mornings, I want to curl up in my duvet and chain myself to the bed. Do you reckon if I swallowed the key to a padlock I would be allowed to stay chained to my bed, in my house? The place I feel safe.

At school Rona could easily come up behind me, and start the bullying. Out there she's the boss. But in my own house I'm the boss. I have doors that can block her off and a mum who would tell her off.

If only school was like that!

Lee came as usual to pick me up. At half past eight, there she was on the doorstep, smiling at me.

"Alright Sam?" she said, giving me a quick hug. I avoided her eyes, but I sensed her urge to ask me what had happened yesterday. I knew she wouldn't ask, though. I had to bring it up, that was how our friendship worked. If there was something bothering us we waited to be told exactly what it was. I felt a sudden warm love towards my best friend. Here was the one person I could rely on. I returned her hug, and linked her arm through mine.

"Bye Mum!" I called out as I shut the door.

"Bye love, have a good day," she shouted back. She was listening to Norah Jones again. God, how I hated her music. She had a good voice, but talk about depressing. Lee and I had a nickname for her.

"Snorah Jones," we said, in unison. I laughed and with that we set off for school.

I was in a good mood, but not for long. Walking along, arm in arm with Lee, I was happy, but then we rounded a corner and in front of us was my school. Tall, grey, scabby, old, that just about sums it up. I gave a sigh and Lee gave me a funny look.

"Oh, come on Sam, if Rona's here then just freak her out like you did me yesterday afternoon. That will scare her off!" she teased. I may have been imagining it, but I thought there was a bitter note in her voice.

I smiled. "Mmmm, maybe," I agreed. I started off towards school.

"Sam!" Lee suddenly shouted from behind me. She looked angry and upset about something, but I didn't know what. "Are you seriously not going to tell me about what happened yesterday? I'm your best friend."

"Lee... nothing happened yesterday." I tried.

"Oh, sure. Thanks for confiding in me!" she exclaimed, and with that she turned away, leaving me stood there, rooted to the spot.

What had just happened? I felt tears well up in my eyes. Why was Lee so bitter about this? I walked towards my school, lost in my own thoughts. I was so absorbed with my thoughts that I was completely oblivious to a girl coming up towards me, followed by a group of three girls.

"Well, well, look who it is," drawled a voice behind me. I froze. The cold hand of dread had grabbed me, and I thought I would be sick. "Turn round and look at me when I'm talking to you, Scabby Sam."

I had no choice; I turned round and looked into the face of Rona Fielts. The Year Ten bully and the girl who took pleasure in making my life hell!

I remembered just in time about my mind-reading, and quickly focussed my eyes onto the gorgeously curly blond hair that hung lazily over one shoulder. Rona was the prettiest girl in the school, and she knew it. She had large green eyes with long lashes, golden hair that was always perfect, and creamy skin. Her figure was perfect and she always showed it off with skirts, or low cut school shirts. She had been out with most of the boys in Year Eleven, quite a few Year Twelves, and was currently dating Tom Racher, the tall, dark-haired model, who was 19. He was gorgeous and repulsive from the little I knew of him. He was arrogant, proud, and very rich. This was probably why Rona loved him so much.

"Look me in the eyes, Sam, or are you too pathetic and short to even look that high?" she said, putting on an infuriating baby accent, and pouting her lips. Her friends sniggered in the background and Rona looked pleased. I frantically tried to think of a way out. If I looked her in the eyes I would be filled with her thoughts. I couldn't face having her thoughts in my head. If that happened she would have conquered me altogether. She would be in my private, personal space and she would have finally won.

But then another part of my mind kicked in, telling me that I could use this to my advantage. I thought about that. There was no way I would look Rona in the eyes, but I could look at one of her friends.

I glanced quickly at a girl stood just behind Rona. Her thoughts came flooding into my head, and I hated it. I was a freak! No normal people could read minds. I looked away, but not before some of the girl's thoughts had whispered their feelings to me.

"No. I just don't like the colour of your eyes," I whispered, defiantly.

"What did you say? Only, you're so low down I can't quite hear you," Rona asked, and with that she bent down so she was level with me. That was one thing Rona loved about me, in a twisted kind of way. I was the shortest in the year, which meant she could pick on me about my height. She was the perfect height, everyone knew her, and most people loved her.

I pushed my shoulders back and held my head high. "I said no! Oh, and by the way, your friend behind you thinks you're a stuck-up princess. She hates you and she got off with Tom last night!" I told her. I heard a gasp from the girl and with that I pushed through her and into the school.

I managed to get a few metres before I was overcome with shaking. I had stood up to Rona! I had really done it. But she'd make me pay for that.

Oh, I'd pay dearly for making her look stupid in front of her friends. I dreaded lunch break, but most of all I dreaded what she might do. It would be something bad. I had talked back to Rona, and for that Rona would despise me even more!

Lessons passed quite normally, apart from the fact that Lee refused to talk to me. I lost her at break, and then at lunchtime she sat with some other people she knew. I decided to go home for lunch.

Mum was waiting for me, with some spaghetti on the table. I thanked her and then ate. I wasn't hungry, I felt sick, but Mum mustn't know.

Mum was on my back, trying to talk to me and find out what was wrong, the whole way back to school. She drove me there in our little 'Mini Adventure'. I used to love that car, but it's amazing how quickly you can turn from loving to hating when you're stuck in the car doing 30 miles an hour because that's the fastest it can go.

I shouldn't have minded, but it was getting on my nerves. Everything was annoying me, the slow chugging of the engine, Mum's music, her constant questioning about the day before. "Was my head ok?" "Did I need to take some paracetamol?", "Was everything alright at school?" It was doing my head in. The anger was slowly building up inside me; I was going to explode soon. And then we arrived and Mum was backing away, giving me a cheery wave and driving off, and I was left staring at the playground which was completely empty. Everyone was inside, lunch break had ended, and I was going to be in so much trouble!

I walked into Mr Rimad's class with my head down.

"Sorry I'm late, Sir," I said, looking past his right shoulder. Mr Rimad's mane of light was duller than everyone's in the class I thought, randomly, as I snuck a look at my fellow pupils. Maybe age dims the light. It was interesting, another theory for me to try out. *No!* I thought suddenly. *Forget the mind-reading; it's too weird.*

"Where have you been, Samantha?" he said sternly, jerking me away from my thoughts. I knew he wouldn't accept the slow car story, but what choice did I have?

I got two lunchtime detentions, one for being late, and the other for being cheeky. Apparently coming up with such a lame excuse was rudeness and did I really expect it to be accepted as a genuine reason for arriving to my lesson so late?

I took my seat next to Lee and got out my books. This was not turning out to be a good day at all. I smiled at Lee. "Sorry about this morning," I whispered.

She glared at me. "Then why talk about it behind my back?" she whispered, stonily, and turned her back on me.

"I'll tell you what it's all about this afternoon," I said. What was she on about? Who had been talking about what behind her back?

"Silence, Samantha!" Mr Rimad shouted. I heard someone muffle a laugh behind me. I clenched my fists and looked at Lee and, to my surprise, found her trying not to laugh. I gave her a hurt look and got on with my work. She was shaking beside me with suppressed laughter and it was annoying and upsetting at the same time. I didn't know what she was laughing at, but I didn't know if I wanted to know.

I suddenly remembered my eye contact rule. If I could just look into her eyes for a second, her thoughts would tell me what she was laughing at and they would be out of my head quickly. But I was scared of the fact that I could do this. Why could I suddenly read people's minds? I wanted to forget it. So I didn't read Lee's thoughts. I should have done though; it would have helped me understand what she did next, and why.

******

I waited for her in our usual spot; we always walked home together. But Lee was late. I was worried; she was never late. I hoped she wasn't still mad at me. I had tried to make it up to her. If she couldn't accept my apology then that was her problem. Then she came out of the school. She looked over at me and raised an eyebrow. What was wrong with her? I started over, but then Rona came out and, as though it was the most natural thing in the world, she linked arms with Lee and looked at me.

"What's she doing here, Lee?" she asked. "Nobody likes Scabby Sammy!"

Lee looked at me. She looked slightly awkward. "You don't like Sam, do you?" Rona said suddenly, looking down at Lee. "Well?"

"Er... no, I don't," Lee said, looking everywhere

but where I stood, open-mouthed with shock.

"Lee...?" I whispered.

"Oh, go away Scabby Sammy!" Lee shouted, and with that she and Rona walked off, arm in arm.

I felt as if I'd been kicked in the stomach. I couldn't breathe properly, and my heart was thumping painfully. I was going to cry, but not here where everyone would see. I started to walk home, surrounded by grief.

This day could not get any worse, and then it started to rain. How appropriate! I walked home in the pouring rain, not caring; I was shivering when I got home.

Mum had gone out and left a note on the kitchen table: 'Gone shopping, back later. Love Mum xx'

I dropped my school bag on the floor, and then collapsed into a heap on the floor, crying my eyes out. I had so many feelings swirling around me and the strongest was hurt. Lee was my best friend, and she had just told my enemy that she didn't like me. I felt utterly alone, utterly unloved and completely torn in two. And then these stupid ideas started running through my head. There were knives in the kitchen, big sharp knives. It would be easy to hurt myself. I deserved it. It was seeming like a better and better idea the more I thought about it. But I stayed curled up on the floor, lost in my own thoughts, when a sudden itching on my arm jerked me back to reality.

For some reason, this itch annoyed me and suddenly all the hurt became anger. I dug my nails into my arm where it was itching. It went away, then came back. I started furiously scratching away at my arm.

I ignored the dull pain my nails were making, and was surprised to find that the pain took my mind off my other problems. I suddenly knew why people self-harm. While I was thinking about this, I suddenly realized that my arm was bleeding. I looked and saw that I had scratched away so much skin that I had hit a vein and the skin was red and raw, blood was slowly trickling down my arm, warming it. And that's when I realised how cold I was. I cuddled into myself, crying at the pain in my arm, crying for the bad day I had had.

And that's how Mum found me. Curled up on the floor, shivering and crying and bleeding!

It was while telling Mum everything that had happened that I realized how stupid I had been. The scratching had gone deeper than I had intended, and Mum had been angry with me. She had always been there, and of course she deserved to be told what had been happening. She didn't believe me of course, so I had looked into her eyes. The thoughts had come flooding in. What colour was she thinking of? I told her. What thought was she thinking over and over in her head? I told her again. I answered every question correct, and the shock and wonder on her face told me that she believed me now.

Mum then of course wanted to know everything about it. She had made me explain what it felt like to have other people's thoughts in my head, asked what I could hear. What did the thoughts sound like? Where did my thoughts go? I answered every question I could. Then we cuddled up on the sofa and watched TV. That's what we're doing now. Mum had an idea to watch a program called *Psychic*.

That was the moment that changed my life forever, watching a programme about a man who could read people's minds. That was when I realized I wasn't a freak, I had a chance to change my life, and I would! This man wasn't in a mental home, he was respected and loved. That could be me. No more bullies shoving me around. I was going to make a difference!

******

I woke up the next morning and got ready. For the first time in ages I looked at myself in the mirror. I had long brown hair, blue eyes and a slightly snub nose. I looked so plain, but I had a mane of light around me, and it made me look almost angelic. My mane of light was glowing brightly this morning, and I looked much less boring.

I had a sudden idea. I rushed into Mum's room and got her make-up bag. I carefully applied foundation and bronzer to my cheeks, then I added some eyeliner and mascara and finally some lippy. I looked at my finished reflection; I looked so much better.

I ran down the stairs and out of the door. Lee wasn't waiting for me. I hadn't thought she would be, but it still hurt. She would rather walk with Rona, her new-found best friend. What exactly had I done that had been so bad? I walked to school by myself and got to school five minutes early. I looked round the playground. There was Lee, hanging round with Rona. I walked past without looking at them. I heard Rona say something behind me, but I wasn't going to let it get to me. I walked into the classroom; there were some of the girls from my tutor group sat in the corner having a debate about fox hunting. I decided to risk going over.

"Hi," I said. "Mind if I join you?" I noticed I was biting my nails and quickly stopped, giving them a big smile.

"Yeah, sure," said one of them, a girl named Lucy.

"What's your opinion on fox hunting?" said another one, called Izzie.

"Well, I always thought it looked quite fun…" and with that we were off, I was accepted and we were in a heavy debate when Mr Lukas walked in.

"Quiet, please, everyone!" he said. I got up to go back to my place but Lucy grabbed my arm. "Stay with us, Sam," she said. I smiled. I had some new friends, I sat with them and ate lunch with them, it was only walking home that I was by myself again.

I had had a good day, and then my way was suddenly blocked by Rona. She had a cigarette in her hand and Lee was beside her with a cigarette in her mouth. I stared at her, shocked. Lee had always hated smoking, and found it repulsive. She had changed so much. I had to read her thoughts; I needed to know what I had done.

I looked her in the eyes and her thoughts came flooding in. I welcomed them and that was when I realized that my life had always been missing something and this was it. My mind always was that bit too empty, my thoughts always slightly alone. I laughed out loud, I was so happy, and then I heard Lee's thoughts. *Weirdo!* she was thinking, and also,

I miss being her friend. But she told everybody things and not me! She said I was a freak who had run after her like a madman!

So that was why she was so angry, people had been telling her things, and she had believed them. Lee was so gullible, it was something we often joked about, but now it had ruined our friendship.

I had no doubt about who had told Lee all the lies. And sure enough Rona, right on cue, linked arms with Lee and looked down at me.

"Come on, Lee, maybe Scabby Sam wants to tell her new friends more rubbish about you!"

So she was admitting to my face that she had said it, and she thought I was just going to say nothing.

"You stuck up… selfish pig!" I shouted at her. All the pent-up fury that had been building up inside me suddenly released. "You've sunk far lower than I thought possible, Rona! Telling Lee lies about things I never said!"

Rona was looking outraged and shocked. Lee, I noticed, was looking slightly confused. People had stopped to listen and I noticed some girls starting to form a ring around us. Sure enough, some boys suddenly started shouting, "Cat fight, cat fight!" I knew what I had to do. If I fought her, I would get beaten badly, so I just looked her in the eyes. If I could find something in her memories to use against her then I could win easily.

Rona's thoughts filled my mind and I recoiled in shock. All her thoughts were full of pain. A thought jumped out at me, a memory of her dad throwing a glass bottle at her back, the pain she had felt as the glass cut her skin. There were more of her being thrown against stairs while she watched her dad beat her mum. More thoughts showed me memories of Rona being beaten, sworn at and called nasty things; her thoughts were so full of grief that I felt immediate pity for her. And then her voice came through the thoughts.

"So, Scabby Sammy, what are you gonna do now?"

I looked away from Rona and her thoughts left me. It was a relief and a huge weight off my shoulders. Rona suddenly gave me a huge shove. I stumbled and fell over. My hand caught my fall but there was glass beneath it and I felt a searing pain as a glass shard cut a slash right across my palm. I gasped and looked up at Rona. She was smirking down at me.

I couldn't let her get away with this. She started to walk away. "So this is what it feels like to be hit with glass!" I shouted, before I could stop myself.

She froze. "What did you say?" she said, slowly. She was angry now.

I stood up slowly. What had I said that for? Now she'd give me what for. There was a murmur as everyone saw my cut and bleeding hand. There was a circle of spectators around us now. I held my hand up and let the blood trickle down my wrist.

"It does hurt. Does a glass bottle hurt more, I wonder?" I said. *No Sam, shut up right now*, said another, wiser part of me.

Rona stood there looking shocked. "How the hell do you know that? You don't know anything about me!" Rona exclaimed and then suddenly came over and slapped me round the face. It stung sharply, and throbbed. I grabbed her wrist with my cut hand, it hurt and I let go straight away, leaving a trail of blood, bright red against her pale skin.

Rona looked at it. "Are you crazy?" she shouted.

"No!" I shouted back. She had bullied me, and I wanted to show her that I wasn't afraid any more. "I didn't think you'd mind the sight of blood. You've seen it enough on your mum's face, and yours, probably. Tell me when the last time your dad beat you was? Maybe yesterday? Or this morning even?" I was prepared to hurt her just like she had hurt me.

Sure enough, tears welled in her eyes. She looked completely vulnerable, and suddenly I realized that I was bullying her and I didn't like it. I shouldn't have sunk to her level. I thought desperately.

"What...?" she whispered.

"Your dad beats you up, doesn't he?" I said, before I could help it. I cursed myself silently. She looked at me. "He gets drunk and then beats you and your mum up. So then you come and take it out on me. Not any more! Just 'cause you have a bad life doesn't mean you can bully other kids just to make yourself feel better." I was crying now, not just from anger, but from all the times she had made me feel so bad, and from the fact that I was hurting her so much in return. "Leave me alone from now on, Rona," I said, and with that I walked past her.

I heard her turn behind me and I looked round. She was staring at me. And then, without a word, she reached a sleeve up to her face and wiped off her make-up. There, beneath the foundation, was a big bruise on her cheek.

"You have no idea. You have absolutely no idea," she said, quietly, and then she looked at me. I avoided her gaze; her thoughts were too painful. "You really do have absolutely no idea. You know nothing about me. You think this is going to make it better for you? Well, you just lost the game. There's no way I'm gonna accept you now. You're a freak!" And then she pushed her way through the other pupils and went off crying.

There was silence, and then Lucy and Izzie ran up to me. "Way to go Sam," they said, giving me a hug. Then everyone was talking, congratulating me, going after Rona, and I wasn't able to get away. People were hugging me; one boy even came up to me and told me I looked really nice, and would I go out with him? And then from behind me, someone tugged at my sleeve. I turned round and found Lee looking at the floor.

"I'm... sorry Sam," she whispered. She looked really guilty, and it made me love her instantly. I gave her a hug. This was all I had wanted: Lee as a friend, and us laughing together again. But in the process I had had to hurt Rona, be a bully just like her. In doing what I thought was the right thing, I had become what I most despised. And the reaction I had got just made me feel even worse about it. I had wanted Rona to be angry with me, not upset. The whispered words she had uttered were much worse than if Rona had shouted them. I hadn't meant to hurt her so badly, I had just wanted to be left alone.

I started to walk off. I needed to go home, away

from all this attention, but first I needed to tell Lee everything. So I did. We walked to the park, sat on the swings, and I told her, and she believed me. She didn't try to send me to a loony bin, or stop wanting to be my friend. We walked off arm in arm, she laughed at my jokes, and the stories I had about what I had done with my mind-reading. She told me I looked gorgeous, and then showed me a present she had bought me. It was an eyeshadow kit and an eyeliner.

Just like it used to be, except it was different, she was here talking, laughing with me. But this time, I had other friends. Lee wasn't going to be the only person I could ever talk to, or share things with. I had Lucy and Izzie as well. I walked away from the park with a new life, and it was going to be a better one!

The End

Lauren Child

Lauren Child wrote and illustrated her first children's book, *Clarice Bean, That's Me!* in 1999. She has since written over 16 children's books, including *I Will Not Ever Never Eat A Tomato*, which won the Kate Greenaway Medal. Lauren's first TV series, inspired by the characters *Charlie and Lola*, launched on BBC2 and CBeebies in Autumn 2005.

Ella Bailey

Ella is 14 and lives in Nottingham with her two sisters. Ella is a fan of Lauren Child, Garth Nix and the illustrator Emma Chichester-Clarke. She enjoys playing the guitar and sitting by an open fire on Christmas Eve, watching the snow float down beyond the window. Of writing and illustrating *Oscar and Bella*, she said, "The thing that I enjoyed

most was thinking of all of the different scenarios and adventures I could include in it. The most difficult thing was deciding when to end it."

Oscar and Bella

Ella Bailey and Lauren Child

Oscar was lying on the sofa, idly flicking between TV channels. There wasn't much on – just the usual usual. No one would be home for hours, he would have to make his own tea. It would be fish fingers again. It was only 9.21am, and Oscar had already watched 27 cartoons, eaten five bags of Cheesy Puffs, and run up and down the curtains 14 times precisely. His fizzy drink had run out of fizz, and as he sucked on his straw he wondered what was going on in the world far below. He padded across the floor, stuck his nose up against the glass, and thought, "Wouldn't it be exciting to be one of the people who live outside the window?"

He had never *really* been outside of FLAT 141 Leafy Heights.

Sure, he had been to visit nice Mrs 125's apartment once in a while, he'd whizzed up and down in the elevator probably about a bazillion times – but to Oscar these didn't really COUNT!!!

Especially since Oscar got Bella's umbrella jammed in the doors...!

Bella was Oscar's BEST friend and partner in crime. He went everywhere with her. Everywhere, that is, apart from school. (Oscar didn't do school.)

Which was where Bella just happened to be today. Which was why Oscar just happened to be OH-SO-ALONE in the GIGANTIC flat...

◁ Gigantic here meaning: very very very very very very big!

Bella

It was only Bella's second day at this so-called SCHOOL…

Oscar was already bored stiff as a very stiff plank…

Bella's mummy was nowhere to be seen either – she was at work. It was alright for her, where she was there was always something **NEW** or **EXCITING** going on!

And as for Bella's Dad…

He would be down at the golf course
hitting a little white ball around and yelling,
"Four!" Still – more exciting than what Oscar
was doing.

"Why can't my life be more exciting?" Oscar groaned.

OSCAR

"If you want something doing you better do it yourself," the TV answered.

"Well then, why not?"
Oscar challenged himself.

"You'll never know until you've tried…"

an advert for a new kind of fizzy pop replied.

So Oscar found himself very caught up in the feel of the moment. He also found himself very nervous. Which was silly, of course.
Five minutes later he found himself standing in front of the doors that separated him from the outside world.

He had thought very LONG and HARD about what provisions he was going to need on his expedition. (47 seconds exactly.)
In the end he had packed:

 packets of Cheesy Puffs.

 bottle of fizzy orange, the kind that lets you blow bubbles out of your nose.

 favourite pair of night-vision spy-goggles that made you see everything in green.

A pair of spare socks, just in case the ones he was wearing got wet! (Oscar hated wet socks.)

 another packet of Cheesy Puffs, just in case...

So, with his backpack on his back, and a nervous expression on his face, Oscar took his first step into the outside world…

…and it was quite the most amazing place Oscar had ever been!

Over there was the grocer's. There was the barber's. Bella's dad went to, and just round the corner Oscar found a street lined with shops full of the most extraordinary and expensive garments…

GROCERS

BARBERS

Oscar's mouth watered as he trotted past the café, his nose held high as he breathed deep the smell of the strange and exotic dishes the adults were ordering.

And round here was, er, well it was the grocer's again...

Through the sea of people Oscar tried to spy his own house, standing on tiptoes – but he wasn't quite tall enough.

It was then that Oscar realized he was rather quite lost!

No one stopped to see if he was OK, even when he tried to ask for directions.

"Can you please tell me where Leafy Heights is?" He tried to make himself heard above the crowd, tugging at a businessman's trouser leg. But the businessman didn't stop. He obviously had some important meeting to hurry to.

So there was Oscar, all alone in an absolutely enormous city, and no idea where he was. How he wished he hadn't so impulsively decided to go on an adventure.

"Well it's still more exciting than being stuck in a flat all day!" Oscar thought, as he munched his way through his second packet of Cheesy Puffs and wondered what to do next. It did seem rather silly to want to go back to the flat so soon.

Oscar eventually decided that he better soldier on...

and on...

and on...

and on...

and on for what seemed like absolutely forever.

Until, all of a sudden, he heard a noise behind him. A noise quite different to anything else he had heard in the city before. Oscar looked back over his shoulder, only to see a huge, very ferocious-looking dog bounding along the street, carving a wide path through the alarmed crowd.

Oscar leapt aside just in time. He leapt…

and landed right in an enormous shopping bag (being quite small, he fitted in snugly). A shopping bag belonging to a posh old woman with a fruit bowl on her head, who looked even more ferocious than the ferocious dog! So of course Oscar didn't do anything, as the bag began to sway as the lady carried it along through the crowd.

He just huddled up as small as possible – while nibbling at a bag of peanuts he had found!

Till eventually the bag stopped moving, and Oscar dared peek out.

FLOWERS

The posh old lady was in deep conversation with another posh old lady, who also looked rather ferocious. So Oscar clambered out of the bag as quietly as he could, leaving the empty bag of peanuts behind.

Looking around, Oscar saw he was in a completely different part of town now.

The streets were wider, with far fewer people on them, and the buildings surrounding him were mostly houses with big front gardens.

And there was much less noise here!
Apart from a persistent buzzing!

Wait, not buzzing! Oscar listened hard, heading to where he thought the noise was coming from. It sounded quite like people, lots of people, laughing and shouting – and then as Oscar rounded the next corner he saw it...

He had somehow managed to find his way to the school where, at that precise moment, Bella was enjoying a game of Cops and Robbers with her school friends. Oscar dropped his last packet of Cheesy Puffs and raced towards the fence.

"Bella!" he cried.
"Oscar!" she yelled, "What are you doing here?"
"I got lost!"
"Oh, Oscar!"

Bella hugged him through the iron railings.

"Who are you talking to Bella?" a kind–looking lady asked her.

"Oscar!"

"Oh... is Oscar your imaginary friend?"

"I am no such thing!" Oscar replied indignantly.

The lady just laughed and let him in through the gate.

"So you decided to come to school after all then, Oscar?" Bella asked with a smile.

"Not on purpose!" Oscar said, and he told her all about his utterly amazing day. And what an utterly amazing coincidence it was that he had ended up at Bella's very own school.

"Well, now you're here, maybe you could stay for the rest of the day?" said Bella. "We do colouring and all sorts!"

"Maybe I could!" grinned Oscar.

And maybe he did.

Who knows?

Well, nobody knows what Oscar gets up to – except Bella!

The End

Runners-up

Aaron Brown • Abaigh McKee • Abigail Watt • Abubakr Karbhari • Adam Feltham • Adanna Ehirim • Aedryan Chklar • Ailsa Purdie • Aimee Blackman • Aimee Wilmot • Alana Gladwish • Alastair MacKinnon • Alex Barrett • Alex Gelder • Alex Jackson • Alex Maxwell • Alice Bennett • Alice Dewa • Alice Newton • Alice Oatway • Alice Thornton • Alice Uggles • Alice Walker • Alison Lannon • Alissa Cooper • Amanda Lynch • Amberlie Hyde • Amelia Bain-McCullough • Amy Bretherton • Amy Brownlee • Amy Harrison • Amy Layton • Amy Trinh • Amy Trollope • Ana Fernandez • Andrew Bedford • Andrew MacDonald • Anna Davies • Anna Dewolf • Anna Garrett • Anna James • Anna Mitchyn • Anna Pope • Anna Radford • Anna Ryland-Jones • Annabel Knowles • Areeb Siddiqui • Aryan Ghorashi • Ashleigh Cook • Ashleigh Maskell • Ashlyn Tegg • Ashwin Sharma • Becky Adcock • Ben Atkinson • Ben Lane • Benjamin Holton • Beth Stout • Bethanie Murray • Bethany Aitman • Bethany Brant • Bethany Harris • Bethany Hawkins • Bethany Jones • Bethany Knott • Bethany Morledge • Bethany Seale • Bethany Shiers • Bethany Woods • Bilqees Baseer • Brendan Elmes • Brendan Selkirk • Brook Halfpenny • Browwen Fraser • Caitlin Ryan • Cara Fachau • Caragh Jones • Carim Nahaboo • Carys Jones • Catherine Corry • Catherine Honor • Catherine Mortimer • Catherine Nettleship • Catherine Prior • Catherine Saunders • Catriona Aldrich-Green • Catriona Bolt • Charlotte Gilbert • Charlotte Leatherby • Charlotte O'Carroll • Charlotte White • Chloe Jeffries • Chloe Penston • Chloe Watson • Chris Hickey • Christine Murphy • Christopher Davis • Christopher Watson • Christopher Woodhouse • Ciara Elwis • Claire Gisler • Claire Walmsley • Clare Coggins • Conor Giles • Corinna Murray • Daisy Nash • Daisy Rodman • Dan Hooke • Daniel Brown • Daniel Laycock • Daniel Middleton • Daniel Thompson • Danielle Drury • Danielle O'Brien • David Gundry • David Guppy • David Haworth • David Owen • Deanna Turnbull • Dickie Chan • Dominic Spillane • Donna Norris • Elinor Cooper • Eliza Burt • Elizabeth Arscott • Elizabeth Randall • Ella Ungless • Ellen Hughes • Ellen Pearce • Ellie Bishop • Ellie Morris • Ellie Phillpotts • Ellie Smith • Ellie Tonks • Ellie Wonnacott • Elliott Brattinga • Elliw Evans-Jones • Elyse MacKinnon • Emily Beevers • Emily Goodaker • Emily Hancock • Emily Metcalfe • Emily Nash • Emily Ramsden • Emily Slade • Emily Tridimas • Emily Vernall • Emily White • Emily Wright • Emma Gainford • Emma Hardy • Emma McLean • Emma Ryder • Erin Packer • Eryn Russell • Esther Jourdan • Ethan Jeffrey • Eva Crean • Eve Bayram • Faye Thompson • Felice Laake • Felicity Edwards • Felicity Juckes • Felix Thompson • Flora Loughridge • Frances Cunningham • Frances Reed • Francesca Clavsen •

Francesca Dorricott • Francis Dunnett • Francis Kermani • Freya Matthews-Jones • Freya Moar-Smith • Gabriel Cagan • Gemma Cantwell • Gemma Carr • Gemma McLean • George Simonds • Georgia Hutchinson • Georgia Tomlinson • Georgina Canty • Georgina Coles • Georgina Ling • Geraint Ellis • Grace Andrews • Grace Butcher • Grace Cherry • Grace Hodgson • Hannah Bennett • Hannah Gornall • Hannah Henretty • Hannah Levy • Hannah Pollard • Hannah White • Harriet Lowe • Harriet Reed • Harriet Wakeman • Harry Beal • Hattie Rees • Hayley Irons • Hazel Young • Heather Eddas • Heather Marlow • Heidi Simms • Helen Rockliff • Helen Saunders • Helena Kaczmarska • Helena Raymond-Hayling • Helena Shears • Holly Duddell • Holly Gilmour • Hugo Humpidge • Imogen Gerard • Imogen Lepere • Imogen Taylor • Iona Cloran • Isabel Terrell • Isabelle Barrett • Isla Williams • Isobel Edwards • Jack Hinchey • Jack Sargeant • Jacob Atherton • Jacob Close • Jake Shackleford • Jake Toulouse-Lisle • James Denton • James Fretwell • James Kenny • James Patterson • Jane Savage • Jaqui Howard • Jaquie Peate • Jasmine Walter • Jasmine Weyer-Brown • Jason Vallance • Jayne Coffey • Jennifer Anderson • Jenny Shelley • Jess Wood • Jessica Finn • Jessica Francis • Jessica Hemming • Jessica Kempster • Jessica Miller • Jessica Perviz • Jessica Rose • Joanna Birch • Joanna Cockerill • Joe Davey • Joel Tiley • John Kuzminski • John Lavery • Jonathan Jarvis • Josh Bale • Josh Barlow • Josh Cork • Josh Lucas • Joshua Carr • Joshua Mitchell • Josie Fryers • Joss Marshall • Julia Walmsley • Kate Atkinson • Kate Davies • Kate Docking • Kate Evans • Kate Paxton • Kate Sheppard • Katharine Langham • Katherine Weekes • Kathryn Adams • Kathy Cox • Katie Knowles • Katie Perridge • Katie Pickup • Katie Saker • Katy Pilkington • Kayleigh Johnson • Keeley Dalton • Kerensa Gaunt • Kiran Cunningham • Kiran Dhiman • Kirath Bharya • Kirsty Laurenson • Kylie Moor • Laura Alison • Laura Bareham • Laura Bartlett-Short • Laura Cross • Laura Longworth • Laura Newman • Laura Robinson • Laura Rolinson • Laura Rowson • Laura Simpson • Laura Weatherby • Lauren Cooper • Lauren Davidson • Lauren Hay • Lauren Jack • Lauren McFerran • Lauren Quinton • Lauren Saunders • Lauren Stevens • Layla Fazal • Leah Williams • Leonie McQuillan • Lester Talbot • Liam Godfrey • Lilleth Lawton • Lindsay Unwin • Lisa Ward • Lizzie Rudin • Lois Townsend • Lorna Mann • Lorna Martin • Louise Cormie • Louise Hall • Louise Merrington • Louise Miller • Lucy Davidson • Lucy Furneaux • Lucy Marshall • Lucy Whitehouse • Lydia Mackay • Lydia McGill • Lydia Sawyer • Macrae Williams • Maddi Williams • Maddie Sharman • Maddy Pledge • Madeleine Winnard • Malini Dey • Mandeep Matharu • Marianne Murray • Martha Lawless • Marwa Amar • Mashal Iftikhar • Matthew Byrne • Matthew Kinloch • Matthew Mitchell • Matthew Turner • Matthew Young • Mavra Mirza • Meagan Boyd • Megan Bradbury • Megan Gough • Megan Haward • Megan Moore • Megan Thomas • Mia Thomas • Michael Boniface •

Michael Turner • Mina Ghosh • Mollie Claaseu • Molly Bradshaw • Molly Garnett • Molly Lyon • Molly Richardson • Molly Silk • Naazneen Pathan • Nadia Howard • Nancy Wesby • Naomi Hanna • Naomi Winter • Natalie Birmingham • Natalie Brown • Natasha Jeacock • Nathan Jackson • Niall O'Donahue • Nicholas Gott • Nicola Cave • Nicola Risbridger • Nikki Woolmer • Ninah Richards • Nisha Haq • Noor Ramadan • Nuala Kelly • Olaolu Adeboye • Oliver Comins • Olivia McCarthy • Paige Fletcher • Patricia Readom • Penny Sheard • Phillip Skippon • Phoebe Crompton • Phoebe Power • Pippa Smith • Polly Burns • Rachael Midlen • Rachael Wootton • Rachel Dennis • Rachel Ellis • Rachel Hodkinson • Rachel Leeson • Rachel Loosley • Rachel Maddocks • Rachel Preston • Rachel Ross • Rachel Speirs • Rachel Summers • Rachel Taylor (Cheshire) • Rachel Taylor (Kent) • Rajpal Chahal • Raunaq Latif • Raveena Virdee • Ray Otsuki • Rebecca Davies • Rebecca Maltman • Rebecca Morgan • Rebecca Morton • Rebecca Phillips • Rebecca Pizzey • Rebecca Priest • Rebecca Whitter • Rebecca Wilmot • Rebecca Wright • Rebekah Watts • Reem Al-Ajeel • Rhian Fender • Rhiannon Slatcher • Rianne Fitzpatrick • Rob Scothern • Robert Spooner • Robert Torn • Robyn Shields • Roisin Convery • Rosamund Downer • Rosie Greening • Rosie Lord • Rosie McNamara • Rowena Hargill • Roxanna Shamim Ahmad • Ruby Emmott-Dixon • Rukayat Lawla • Ruth Allen • Ruth Malcolm • Ryan Barker • Saara El-Arifi • Safian Younas • Safiya Sheikh • Sairah Shah • Sam Burr • Sam Fish • Sam Reinders • Samantha Boland • Samantha Burstow • Samantha Quinn • Samantha Shelley • Samuel Morris • Samuel Wakley • Sarah Anderson • Sarah Dignan • Sarah Haynes • Sarah Hickin • Sarah Holdaway • Sarah Kenchington • Sarah McKenna • Sarah Reed • Sarah Jane Carson • Sarra Gray • Sasha Reid • Sean Howson • Sebastian Ritchie • Serena Connelly • Shannon Murphy • Shayda Karimi • Sian Avery • Sophie Cox • Sophie Gardiner • Sophie Hallewell • Sophie Harding • Sophie Hewitson • Sophie Hyde • Sophie Jackson • Sophie Madden • Sophie Payne • Sophie Shaw • Sophie Szynaka • Stephanie Foster • Stephanie Leddington • Stephanie Tattersall • Stephen O'Sullivan • Susan Xia • Tayiab Mahmood • Thomas Hulley • Timothy Carsons • Toby Comer • Tom Blatherwick • Tom Emms • Tom Ward • Tracie Pooler • Twinkle Darnley • Victoria Bremner • Victoria Holdstock • Viki Gardiner • Will Ford • Yashaswini Choudhary • Yuhan Hu • Zara Bhatti